On the Edge

D0230159

Other books by Gillian Cross

For younger readers

GILLIAN CROSS

On the Edge

OXFORD
UNIVERSITY PRESS

OXFORD
UNIVERSITY PRESS

Great Clarendon Street, Oxford OX2 6DP

Oxford University Press is a department of the University of Oxford.
It furthers the University's objective of excellence in research, scholarship,
and education by publishing worldwide in

Oxford   New York

Auckland   Cape Town   Dar es Salaam   Hong Kong   Karachi
Kuala Lumpur   Madrid   Melbourne   Mexico City   Nairobi
New Delhi   Shanghai   Taipei   Toronto

With offices in

Argentina   Austria   Brazil   Chile   Czech Republic   France   Greece
Guatemala   Hungary   Italy   Japan   Poland   Portugal   Singapore
South Korea   Switzerland   Thailand   Turkey   Ukraine   Vietnam

Oxford is a registered trade mark of Oxford University Press
in the UK and in certain other countries

Copyright © Gillian Cross 1984

The moral rights of the author have been asserted

Database right Oxford University Press (maker)

First published 1984
First published in this edition 2004

First published in this paperback edition 2000

All rights reserved. No part of this publication may be reproduced,
stored in a retrieval system, or transmitted, in any form or by any means,
without the prior permission in writing of Oxford University Press,
or as expressly permitted by law, or under terms agreed with the appropriate
reprographics rights organization. Enquiries concerning reproduction
outside the scope of the above should be sent to the Rights Department,
Oxford University Press, at the address above.

You must not circulate this book in any other binding or cover
and you must impose this same condition on any acquirer

British Library Cataloguing in Publication Data
Data available

ISBN 978 0 19 275371 7

3 5 7 9 10 8 6 4 2

Printed in Great Britain by
Antony Rowe Ltd, Chippenham, Wiltshire

Paper used in the production of this book is a natural, recyclable
product made from wood grown in sustainable forests. The
manufacturing process conforms to the environmental regulations
of the country of origin.

Day One — Sunday 7th August

11.00 a.m.

He seemed to have been running for ever, his feet thudding
down on to the pavements, his eyes stinging as the sweat
dripped into them. Every muscle ached to stop, to give up. It
was only his brain that kept him going. That and the steady
bleep bleep bleep of the pacemaker on his watch.

He came round the last corner just as the church bells
started up, and saw his own front door, a hundred metres
ahead. His breathing had almost given out, his feet were
losing their rhythm and his throat tightened, making him gag.
But he couldn't give up. Not now. He had decided to do five
miles and five miles was what he would do. He screwed up
his mind deliberately, to the last effort, and stared hard at the
yellow door. And suddenly the church bells and the blood
thudding in his ears and his grinding determination all came
together, melting into a great wave of joy and certainty. He
kicked for home and his legs, which had been at the end of
their strength, seemed to flood with new power so that they
took him as if he were flying, until he stumbled up the front
path and flopped against the door. Then he looked down at
his watch.

Done it! Thirty-six minutes twenty seconds. He had
broken thirty-seven minutes at last. Pressing the button to
change from the stop-watch display to the time, he reached
for the key hanging round his neck. A hot bath. That was
what he needed. He could soak for as long as he liked, with
no one to fuss him. And when his mother finally got home
they would have a slap-up meal. Today she was due to make
some big breakthrough in her latest investigation and she had

promised him steak and chips and a fantastic cream gateau. That should get his strength back. Grinning, he turned the key in the lock and pushed the door open.

As he did so, he was gripped by a primitive, uneasy feeling. Dark! The house was too dark, as though all the curtains were drawn. And there was something else . . . . But exhaustion dulled his reactions and all he did was stretch out a hand towards the light switch.

Then everything crashed round him. No light. Instead, from behind, from the other side of the door, a body launched itself. An arm went chokingly round his neck and a hand pressed against his face, forcing a pad over his nostrils.

Fight! said his brain.

But he had nothing left. His muscles gave way and he fell, like a pile of wooden bricks pushed over by a baby. He must have knocked his watch, because the last sound he heard was the *bleep bleep* of the pace-maker. Then the darkness swallowed him.

Day Two — Monday 8th August

2.00 a.m.

Fifteen hours later and a hundred and sixty miles away, Jinny Slattery stepped out into the Derbyshire night and sniffed the wind. It smelt of dung and dirty straw, with an undertone of cabbages. Utterly familiar. Even in total darkness she would have known exactly where she was standing. Between the shippon and the pig-crew, with the wind blowing over from the vegetable ground.

But it was not quite dark. The moon was pale and almost full behind a straggle of cloud and the buildings stood round her like sharp-edged cut-outs. Barn, tool-house, pig-crew, shippon, milking-house, dairy. Three sides of a square, with the house as the fourth side. Like a toy farmyard.

And out beyond, across the dale, the great gritstone mass of the Edge loomed dark against the sky. There was not light enough to make out where fields gave way to open heather moor, nor to see the line of bare, rocky crags below the ridge. But even in the half-dark, the Edge possessed the dale, marking out its horizon in a huge sweep from the dale head in the north to the southern end, where the Castle Rock hunched blacker than the night.

Jinny padded over the dusty concrete and out beside the tool-house, on to the rough track that led to the road. Fear kept her alert, like an animal, so that everything was sharper and clearer than normal. When the church clock struck two, from the village down the dale, the cracked, flat notes made her jump.

When she reached the tangle of elders where the track

joined the road, her father stepped out of the shadows and laid a hand on her shoulder.

'Jin.'

She squeaked with surprise, and felt annoyed with herself. 'Made me jump.'

'Ssh!' Joe gripped her arm and for a second she felt his fingers on her wrist, checking her pulse. Then he nodded. 'You'll do. Come on.'

That was all he said. The next moment he had gone, turning left up the road, away from the village and towards the dale head. *Gipsy Joe Slattery*, thought Jinny, remembering the nickname his friends in London had given him. In the shadows she could not see the long, straight hair, slicked back behind his ears, nor the single gold ear-ring he wore. But as he slid along close to the wall, with Ferry the dog at his heels and the bundled net making a hump on his shoulder, he was like the gipsy of everyone's day-dreams. She tried to imitate his movements as she followed him, concentrating on speed and silence and running over and over what she was going to do. So that there should be no mistakes.

Near its head, the dale forked. The road followed the right hand arm, climbing up towards the moorland. But Joe took the rough track on the left that went into the other arm, Back Clough Dale. Jinny followed, trying to keep pace with him as the track grew steeper. He did not wait for her until he reached the highest point of the path, where it tipped over before it ran down into the hollow at the top of the little dale. He put a hand on Ferry's head and stood motionless until Jinny caught up.

Ahead of them, in the hollow, was the old cottage that Mrs Hollins kept for renting out. It squatted low, almost hidden by clustering trees. In daylight, Jinny would have been able to see its grey roof between the leaves, but now there was only a clot of deeper darkness to show where it lay.

Joe took her on five or six steps more and then stopped short beside the five-barred gate. The gate they had chosen. Jinny swallowed hard, her throat suddenly very dry.

8

Putting a finger to his lips, Joe waved a hand at the field beyond the gate and stuck his thumb up. Jinny could not see his expression, but she knew what he meant. He had been round the field in the twilight, long before he met her, blocking off the gaps in the wall. In every squeeze-stile, every place where the stones had been tumbled, he had crammed branches and bushes, so that now there was only one exit. The gate where they were standing. Jinny swallowed again.

Joe slipped the bundled net off his back and began to unroll it, spreading it across the gate and looping it over the top. His fingers moved with a craftsman's sureness, deft even in the dark. Still without speaking, he prodded Jinny, showing her the heap of stones stacked ready under one of the hawthorn bushes beside the gate. She nodded and bent to help him. One row of stones along the top bar of the gate to hold the net in position. Another row of stones along the bottom of the net, on the ground. To make the trap secure. When it was done, the meshes hung treacherously invisible, shivering slightly in the wind. It was so dark that Jinny could hardly see the delicate movements of Joe's hand as he tested every gap, checking that there was no way through.

Then he stood up, scooping Ferry into his arms and dropping him over the gate. He was about to vault over himself when he tensed, one hand on the top bar.

From the road came the sound of a car driving up the dale. At first the wind masked it, but the noise sharpened as it came nearer, swelling through the darkness. When it reached the fork in the dale it slowed suddenly. Then, taking them both by surprise, it turned and came towards them, up the track.

Joe's arm thudded against Jinny's chest, forcing her back under the branches of the hawthorn. Twigs scratched her face and pulled at her plait. Ferry growled once and then was silent. Joe, cowering back under the opposite bush, had thrust a hand round the side of the net and clamped his fingers over the dog's muzzle.

The car laboured over the rough track, bumping into the

ruts. They saw its headlights first, tilted upwards, sweeping the sky with a brilliance that made everything else utterly black. Then it reached the highest point and the light caught the surface of the ground, picking out every tussock and pot-hole with eerie sharpness. For an instant Jinny saw Joe's face, pale and tense, eyes closed against the glare.

Then the car was rumbling past them, the spinning wheels on a level with their faces, throwing up dust. Jinny closed her eyes.

Please God, let them not see us.

When she opened her eyes again, the tail-lights were glowing ahead, dull red. She saw them for a moment more and then they vanished as the car bumped down into the hollow, to the cottage at the end of the track.

Jinny heard the creak of brakes, the opening and shutting of a door. Then a low murmur of voices. It was impossible to make out the words, but a man's voice answered a woman's. Feet tramped and the cottage door opened, grating as it scraped against the floor inside.

Very slowly, Joe crawled across in front of the gate and put his mouth to Jinny's ear.

'Tourists.'

'What do we — ?' she whispered.

But he cut her off short, with a hand over her mouth, 'Wait.'

After a few moments, the boot of the car slammed and a grinding noise drifted up from the hollow, mixing with the stir of branches rustling in the wind. Jinny saw Joe's head cock sideways, to catch the noise, and she puzzled too, trying to identify it. It sounded — yes, that was it — like something heavy being dragged across the stony yard in front of the cottage. She peered down the track, straining her eyes, but there was nothing to see except the trees.

Then the lights were switched on in the house. For a moment or two the trees were lit up eerily all round, until the curtains were pulled.

Jinny relaxed backwards against the bush. Her mind had drifted a little from what they were doing. *I never knew Mrs*

10

Hollins had let this year, she thought. *Keith never said.* And she felt a twist of annoyance. Because she liked everything to be organized and settled. And known to herself.

Joe pushed his watch under her nose, bringing her back to the present.

'We'll give them half an hour to settle,' he breathed.

Together they watched the seconds pulsing slowly, slowly on the watch. Watched the digits change, minute by minute. Until it seemed that they had sat there in the dew for ever, with the hawthorns scratching them and Ferry standing like a stone on the other side of the gate.

But there were no more sounds from the cottage, and, at the end of the half hour, Joe straightened. His fingers touched Jinny's cheek, not kindly but hard. *Remember*, that touch meant. *Remember everything I told you to do.*

Jinny nodded. As if she could forget! She had been rehearsing it in her head all day, while she planted out lettuces and hunted for eggs. Then Joe had gone. Soundlessly over the gate and into the field, sliding along the line of the wall with Ferry behind him.

Jinny stood up, leaning against the gatepost as her right leg tingled with pins and needles. She was shivering now, not from cold but from excitement and fear.

Across the field she heard a faint rustling as Joe and Ferry worked their way round to the far side. Nervously she raised her head and, in that instant, the image of the hare jumped into her brain.

Lying in its usual place. Disturbed already by the noise of the car. Now it was sensing the shadows that went slinking round by the wall. At any moment it would jerk upright to sit crouched on its back legs, muscles taut, ready for danger.

As though it were there in front of her, she saw the pricking of the long ears, their black tips merging into the darkness. Saw the twitching of the soft, sensitive nose. And the big, luminous eyes, staring into the night as every blade of the fur quivered.

Now it would be on its feet, moving uneasily away from

the sound of man and dog, searching out first one hole in the wall and then another. And finding them blocked.

Don't be soft, she scolded herself.

Now there was only one possible way out. And the man and the dog were sweeping closer. Jinny could feel the big, golden eyes turning towards the gate and suddenly — panic. The powerful thrust of the back legs. The black and white flash of a tail as it broke cover and raced for escape, towards the gate.

I can't do it, said the voice in Jinny's head.

But she had to do it. It was part of life. Part of survival and winning your own food. *Never rely on anyone else,* Joe said. *Make sure you can do everything yourself.* Only — suppose you couldn't? Suddenly, Jinny knew that, at the first sound of the hare's running feet, she would shout aloud and make it turn back.

I can't do it!

But there was no sound of running. She did not hear it coming at all. Only a sudden rustle at her feet and the bump of the stones falling off the gate. Falling as the hare leaped between the bars of the gate and slammed into the net.

Even while her brain shouted *I can't* for the last time, Jinny's arms moved automatically, as she had practised in her mind. Her left hand fumbled to feel the shape of the furry head. Her open right hand chopped down sideways, the edge crashing against the hare's neck, where the frail spinal cord ran up through the delicate bones. And the hare's body slumped, warm and dead, against her ankles, still twitching.

She looked down and swallowed hard. Not quite sure what she felt like. And before she could make up her mind, Joe appeared out of the darkness.

'O.K?' his voice was sharp.

'Of course.'

'Good girl.' He bent and disentangled the hare, picking it up by its ears. 'Hold this while I roll the net.'

Jinny hesitated and he pushed the hare at her, frowning until she took it. Her fingers closed round the ears — and nearly dropped them again. Because at that second, a loud, harsh sound broke the silence. Hammering. The noise of metal on metal.

'What on *earth* — ?' Jinny jerked round. But Joe did not falter. His hands went on rolling the net, neat even when he was working fast.

'Nothing to do with us,' he said shortly.

That was what he always said. As though you could ignore the rest of the world and pretend that nothing existed outside the Slattery family. Only this time he was wrong. The hammering went on, irregular and loud.

'It *is* to do with us,' she muttered. 'That racket'll bring the whole world up here. We'll get caught.'

'Rubbish!' Joe stood up, looping the rolled net over his shoulder. 'The hollow shuts the noise in. I'll bet you can't hear a twitter outside Back Clough Dale.'

'But — '

'Come *on*, girl.' He pushed roughly at her, to get her moving. Then he checked himself. 'I reckon you did a fair job just now. No mithering, no fuss. Proper Slattery.'

As he spoke, the hammering faltered. Stopped for a second and started again with a slightly altered note.

Not Slattery all through, thought Jinny. She wanted to know what was going on. It was queer enough for folk to come in the middle of the night. But to come so late and then to set to hammering? What kind of holiday was that? How *could* Joe ignore it?

He was right about one thing, though. As she followed him down the track, she heard the noise of the hammering fade fast. By the time they reached the road, it was just another wisp of sound, mixing with the wind in the trees and the bleating of distant sheep. Hardly noticeable.

Just another secret of the night. Like the dark figures who crept down the dale, carrying a poacher's net and the body of a hare.

10.00 a.m.

It was another seven hours before Tug woke, inside Back
Clough Dale Cottage. The morning sun sho   through the
glass and fell warm on his eyelids, and into his sleep came the
clash and thud of a brass band. Automatically his brain, as it
swam up out of darkness, began to set words to the tune.

> *Weel* may the *keel* row,
> The *keel* row, the *keel* row,
> *Weel* may the *keel* row . . . .

He opened his eyes and saw—nonsense.
Black lines. Heavy, sharp-edged. Criss-crossing over a pale,
bright background. A barred rectangle, slightly askew and
meaning nothing. Black against pale blue. Dark against
light.

> . . . The *keel* row, the *keel* row . . . .

He lay still, his eyes focusing and relaxing, waiting for the
strange dream to go away so that he could wake up properly,
to his own bed in his own bedroom.
But it did not happen. His mind grew clearer and clearer,
but still the strange, black pattern stayed above his head and
the rhythm of the black lines was repeated in his head by the
loud clash of the cymbals and the kettledrums.

> . . . As *I* came through *Sandgate*,
>   Through *Sandgate*, through *Sandgate* . . . .

He blinked and tried to shut out the sound, turning his
head slowly to one side and then the other, attempting to
work it out.
He was lying on his back, looking up at a window — a
skylight — set in a sloping roof. The roof of an attic, perhaps.
Heavy, black bars were fixed across the skylight. Somewhere,

14

very close, turned up to full volume, someone was playing a recording of brass band music.

Blinking again, he rolled over on to his side and suddenly jerked wide awake when he saw the woman leaning against the door. She was not particularly young, around thirty or so, but she looked extraordinary to him. Quite unlike any other woman he had ever seen.

Everything about her was long and stringy. Long legs, long brown hair scragged back into an elastic band, and long, hard fingers that picked restlessly at an edge of the wallpaper. But it was her eyes that got him. Big, light hazel eyes. Almost golden. Staring steadily and warily towards him, without blinking.

When she saw him move, her fingers snapped tight into fists and she stood up straight and said something. But he could not make out the words above the strident music.

> . . . through *Sand*gate
> De *dah* de *dah* de *dah*.

'Sorry?' His voice came out as a croak. He coughed and then spoke louder. 'I couldn't hear you.'

Impatience flickered across her face. Jamming her hands into the pockets of her jeans, she bounced springily from foot to foot and shouted at him. 'I *said*, how are you *feeling?*'

Tug levered himself up and moved his head. The ache that washed around the back of it nearly made him sick. It was as though someone had jumped up and down on the nape of his neck. Every metallic beat of the music made it worse. Pulling a face that was meant to describe all that, he yelled, 'What happened?'

The woman stopped in mid-bounce and the big, golden eyes narrowed as she came closer. 'You don't remember?'

He tried. Pushing his mind backwards over the hump of sleep, through the barriers of headache and noise. He remembered being at home. Opening the front door and — and — and then everything stopped. There was something

15

else after that. Something black and sudden and dangerous. But his brain shied away from it, switching off automatically every time he got near. If only his head did not ache, if only the music would stop, then perhaps he could work it out. But not here like this. He could not snatch at the details he wanted, and all he was left with was the feeling that he had to be careful. No reasons. Just a feeling.

'I don't remember this place,' he said craftily, to test the woman. Actually, he was certain that he had never seen it before in his life. If she tried to pretend anything different, he would know that he could not trust her.

But her reply was unhesitating and casual. So casual that Tug could not catch all the words above the noise. 'Of course . . . when we came here you fell . . . out cold . . . like a fish on a slab . . . nearly ruptured· ourselves carrying you up . . . .'

It was *important* and he couldn't hear. The strain of trying made him feel panicky. Sitting up straight, he bellowed at her. 'The music's too loud! Please turn it off! We can't talk.'

She must have heard him perfectly, because she was quite near and he said it at the top of his voice, but she did not seem to register the words. Instead, she spun away from him and went swinging across the room to the door. As she opened it, the music blasted louder, almost drowning her yell. 'Hey!'

From somewhere below, there was a sound of feet climbing the stairs. Thudding on bare treads, keeping time with the beat of the band. (. . . *keel* row, the *keel* row, the *keel* row . . . .) Not hurrying.

The man who eventually came into the room did not look as though he ever hurried. He was about the same age as the woman, but where she was tense and fidgety, full of suppressed energy, he was perfectly controlled. Under his thick, black hair his face was startlingly white, with pale, cold, blue eyes and light eyebrows. The contrast was almost shocking, as though the warmth of the face had drained upwards, leaving the features frozen. He did not bother to speak, but simply looked towards the woman, raising one

16

eyebrow. Moving over to him, she began to murmur in his ear.

This is ridiculous, Tug thought. He leaned back against the wall and stared at the two of them, the woman swaying slightly, her weight on the balls of her feet, and the man very still. 'Look,' he said. He was trying to sound as polite and reasonable as he could, but the effort of speaking above the music strained his voice. 'You don't understand. I don't remember *anything*. I don't know what's happened or where I am or how I got here. And I don't know who you are. *Please will you tell me what's going on?*'

The woman took a quick, springy step towards him, but the man put a hand on her wrist, stopping her. Then he walked across to the bed and stood over Tug, looking down at him. 'Don't get worked up.' His cold, flat voice sliced through the noise. 'You've had a knock on the head and it's made you forget a few things. No big deal. You'll be fine when you've had some rest.'

He turned as if to go, and Tug panicked. Reaching forwards, he caught at the man's arm. 'You've got to tell me *something!* I don't even know where I am!'

There was a tiny pause, full of the band's blare, and then the man said, 'We're in our cottage that we've rented for the holiday. In Derbyshire. Or have you even forgotten we were coming to Derbyshire?' Firmly he twisted Tug's fingers off his arm, one by one. 'Now try and sleep.' He moved across to the door.

Try and *sleep?* It was like a taunt. Tug swung his legs out of bed. 'I want to know who you are!'

The two of them were already outside on the landing. The man stopped, with his hand on the door-latch and almost smiled. But only one word of what he said carried to the bed. '. . . mirror . . . .'

Then he was gone. Tug hit the door ten seconds too late. When he lifted the latch and pushed, it opened a centimetre and no more. Squatting down, he peered through the narrow crack and saw what was hanging

17

outside across the opening. A heavy padlock, snapped shut. A padlock.

All at once, he was very cold and still. The desperation that had carried him across the room seeped away instantly, like water into sand. In the middle of the vast trumpeting and drumming that washed through the door to torment his aching head, a terrible silence filled his mind. Because until then, ever since he opened his eyes, he had assumed that there was some kind of mistake. That if only he could get them to listen to him and answer his questions he would understand what was going on.

But there was no mistake about a padlock. The person who put that on had meant him to stay shut in. Whether he wanted it or not. So what did he do now?

He knew what he felt like doing — climbing back into bed, pulling the covers up over his head and waiting for everything to get back to normal. For the police or the U.S. Cavalry or the whole army of angels to come sweeping in and whisk him back to real life. Only he was a bit old to believe in fairy godfathers and he had a nasty feeling that this *was* real life. From now on. Take it or — take it. The only choices he had were to try and stay sane or to creep into a corner and start chewing the wallpaper. And he didn't like the look of those little blue flowers crawling up the walls.

He stood up. Right, then. If the door was a No Exit the first thing was to examine the rest of the room.

It was an attic all right. Sloping ceiling and irregular walls, all covered with the blue-flowered wallpaper. The only furniture was the bed, a chest of drawers on one side of the door and a wardrobe on the other. Nothing else except a plastic jug of water on the chest of drawers and a plastic bucket with a lid, down on the far side of the bed. Tug lifted the lid and smelt the disinfectant that lay in a thin layer on the bottom of the bucket, and he felt a sudden twitch of fear. He could guess what the bucket was for. That meant that they weren't going to let him out of the room for *anything*. And they had planned it like that. He breathed faster, and looked round the room again. Nothing to use as a weapon and no way out except the door and the skylight.

He knew already that the door was a dead loss. Climbing on to the bed, he discovered that his head was almost on a level with the skylight. He could reach up and grasp the metal grid.

Not that that was any use. The grid was made of thick bars and it was attached by heavy staples hammered into the window frame all the way round. They had obviously been put there very recently. The bare patches where the hammer had knocked the paint off the wood were fresh and pale. Tug gripped the bars and shook, but nothing moved. Even if he swung on the grid with his whole weight, there was no chance of pulling it away.

But he could wriggle his hand through one of the square gaps between the bars and, by screwing his fingers round, he could open the catch of the skylight and push the window up a little way.

A breath of warm air floated in smelling of dust and summer. By craning his head round to peer through the opening, he could glimpse trees growing, very close, on a steep, upward slope.

Was it really Derbyshire? Perhaps. It might as well have been Kurdistan or Venus for all it mattered. Because he was trapped. Shut up in a strange place with people who would not tell him anything. He was even wearing strange pyjamas — the fluffy, winter kind that he particularly hated.

The noise from outside the door invaded his head constantly, so that he could not begin to work out what was going on. As soon as he tried to clear his mind, the rhythms pounded in, over and over again, identically, so that they must be on a loop of tape. And his brain responded with snatches of words that would not be driven away:

> . . . through *Sand*gate,
> Through *Sand*gate, through *Sand*gate,
> De *dah* de *dah* de *dah*.

He slid down until he was sitting on the bed and went on sliding, so that he curled into a small heap, with his face buried on his knees. He had never imagined that it was possible to feel so frightened and miserable. *Give up*, groaned a voice in his head. *Go back to bed. Pull the covers over your head. There's nothing you can do.*

In that second, when he was right at the bottom, he suddenly thought of Hank. So clearly that he could almost see her little squashed-pekinese face glaring at him. And he knew exactly what she would be screaming:

That's right! Feel sorry for yourself! You're feeble! Look at you! You're not even dressed!

Typical! he snarled back in his mind, just as he would have done if she had been there. *The world's gone mad and you worry about clean socks!*

All the same, he got up — just as he would have done if she had been there — and walked to the chest of drawers. Because there was something cheering about the thought of Hank. Wherever she was, she would not just be sitting back waiting for him to turn up again. And if there were clean clothes in the drawers, he would probably feel better if he put some on. The pyjamas made him feel very vulnerable. He pulled open the top drawer, not expecting much.

And there was his precious Crystal Palace T-shirt. The black one with the blue running-track printed on the front. Tearing off the pyjama jacket, he pulled it over his head. That was better! Rummaging further into the drawer, he found his underwear and socks, but no trousers.

In the wardrobe, perhaps? He spun round and pulled the door open and nearly gave a yelp of delight. Because there, on the floor of the wardrobe, were his trainers. His own, well-worn Nikes, in which he had run so many miles. With those on his feet, he could face anything. He lunged forward to pick them up.

But, as he reached out, something caught his eye. On the inside of the wardrobe door was a full-length mirror. And what was it the man had said? When Tug asked who they were? *Something to do with mirrors.* Slowly, warily he turned.

And for a split second he fell into nightmare. Because the face in the mirror was not his.

Fantastic science fiction stories leaped in his head. Stories of people falling asleep and waking up in someone else's body. But it was only for a split second. Then he realized what was different. His hair. It fell in a thick lock across his forehead, as usual, almost into his eyes. But the colour was wrong. He had expected to see fair hair, almost white. Instead, it was black as ebony — black as the hair of the man who had said 'mirror'. Beneath that black hair, his skin looked startlingly colourless, with pale, cold, blue eyes and light eyebrows. The contrast was shocking. Gazing back at him, the face seemed frozen and stunned.

He went on standing there for a long time, trying not to understand. Not to believe his own eyes. But he could not escape it. With black hair, his pale, blond face looked uncannily like the face of the man who had just gone. He could not remember the features well enough to compare them in detail, but who would notice features when the two of them shared such an extraordinary contrast of colouring?

Almost a family resemblance.

12.45 p.m.

Jinny went scurrying across the farmyard, sending ducks and chickens scattering in all directions. She ran out of the yard and along the track to the road, with the parcel of silver tucked firmly under her arm. The hot sun made her sweat uncomfortably, so that her home-made trousers felt bulky and rough and her shirt clung to her back, but she could not slow down. Joe wanted the parcel sent to the Assay Office as quickly as possible and that meant reaching the village before Mrs Hollins shut the Post Office for lunch.

People stared as she ran into the village and along the main street. Even now, after nine years, they were still curious about the Slatterys and the r strange way of life up the dale. But no one spoke and Jinny was able to ignore them all until she came to the middle of the village. But there, as she might have expected, was Rachel Hollins, sitting in the sun on the wall outside the Post Office. At the very hub of the village where she felt she belonged, with her father the policeman and her mother keeping the Post Office. She was like a sleek kitten, bored and well-fed and ready for mischief, and when she saw Jinny her eyes lit up with happy malice.

'*Jin!* Hallo.' A delicate frown crossed her face, like the cockling of a piece of silk. 'You're not hot? Dressed like that?'

'No,' said Jinny shortly.

Rachel gave an elegant shudder. 'I can't bear to wear a thing but cotton dresses in this weather.' She stroked the exquisite honeysuckle print on her skirt. 'Do you like this one? It's new.'

Jinny wished she could thump her in the chest and knock her backwards into the rose-bed. 'Very pretty. Wouldn't be a lot of use for planting out cabbages though.'

Instantly Rachel's eyes were soft with sympathy. Too soft. 'Oh, I'm *sorry*. I'm clumsy as a cow in wellies. Prinking about my new clothes when you can't have any. And there's you, got to spend all the holidays grubbing round in the mud — '

'There's no mud,' said Jinny. 'It's dry as a bone.'

'Oh, you're so *good!* Never a complaint. And you could have had *everything*. I'll tell you, if my Dad had done that to me I'd — '

Any moment now, Jinny thought, screwing up her fists, *I shall have to hit her.* As she thought it, she heard a car draw up. A car-door slammed and someone walked up behind her.

'Do you never get angry, Jin?' Rachel was saying with relish. 'To think you could have been in London with all the clothes you wanted, and parties and boy-friends and none of this horrible hard work you're forced to do — '

22

Suddenly, miraculously, her voice stopped, in the middle of a sentence. For a second she stared over Jinny's shoulder while her face turned hot pink. Then she jumped off the wall.

'Well, there's no use in chattering here all day. I have to go in to my lunch. I'll tell Keith you're here then?'

'No. Thank you,' Jinny said sweetly. Very aware of whoever-it-was standing behind her. 'I've come for the Post Office.'

She waved her parcel to prove it, but Rachel was already half-way to the house. Jinny grinned. Then she turned round to see who had saved her from any more digs.

And found herself staring into the most extraordinary pair of eyes she had ever seen. Big, pale hazel eyes. Almost golden. Very steady and direct and luminous with the sun that caught them sideways.

Hare's eyes, thought Jinny. And then went pink herself, as though she had said something rude. Because there *was* something hare-like about the woman she was staring at. The elongated face. The long legs. And an odd, sharp alertness, as if those eyes watched for pursuers. Caught off guard, Jinny said the first thing that came into her head.

'Thank you for rescuing me.'

'*You* don't need rescuing,' said the Hare-woman. 'It's that girl who needs it.' She jerked her head the way Rachel had gone. 'Got a mind like a powder-puff.'

Pushing her hands into the pockets of her jeans, she marched up the path into the Post Office. For an instant, Jinny stared after her. It was weird, having a conversation like that with a total stranger. But her eyes . . . . They made you feel that the usual sort of talk was not worth opening your mouth for. No wonder Rachel had choked in the middle of her sniping and jumped off the wall, if those eyes had been staring at her.

The thought of Rachel running away reminded Jinny of her parcel and she scrambled up the path towards the shop door. If she loitered around much longer, Mrs Hollins would come and shut the door in her face.

23

She just slipped in in time. As she crossed the threshold, the pips sounded on the radio for the one o'clock News. Mrs Hollins frowned. Then she walked out from behind the counter and shot the bolts on the door. She was a little woman given to making big gestures. It took her a good ten seconds to turn the OPEN sign to CLOSED. Just to make sure they knew that they were putting her out. Then she looked at Jinny over the Hare-woman's shoulder.

'After Keith, are you? I'll call him.'

'No thank you,' Jinny said politely. Very politely, to try and ward off what was coming next. But it was no use.

'You've never come to spend *money?*' Mrs Hollins mimed exaggerated amazement. 'Well then, I've seen it all. I thought you didn't hold with money, you Slatterys.'

It sounded as though she were teasing. One of those rough jokes that rasped like sandpaper. But Jinny knew better. It was not really so strange, after all, for her to come in with a parcel. All Joe's work had to go to the Assay Office before it was finished. No, what Mrs Hollins wanted — Jinny had seen it all before — was an audience. She was waiting for the Hare-woman to turn round, amused and curious. Ready to be told all about the Slatterys and their peculiar ways. Mrs Hollins loved telling strangers about the Slattery family.

But the Hare-woman did not seem to be paying attention at all. Instead, she was edging over to the far side of the shop, to listen to the News. Wondering what was important enough to save her from Mrs Hollins's jibes, Jinny listened too, catching the news-reader's voice clearly.

Crowds have gathered round the house in Shelley Grove, Hampstead, where terrorists are holding thirteen-year-old Liam Shakespeare, son of journalist and broadcaster Harriet Shakespeare. Police have appealed to people to stay away from the area so that they do not hinder negotiations with the terrorists who are . . . .

24

'There's a terrible thing!' said Mrs Hollins dramatically. 'That poor lad. Just the age of our Rachel. Think if it had been her!'

The Hare-woman, standing with her back to Mrs Hollins, grinned suddenly and gloriously and rolled her eyes up to the ceiling. Jinny almost choked trying to hold her laughter in and Mrs Hollins whirled round at her.

'And what's so funny? Makes you laugh, does it, the thought of that poor boy locked up with maniacs?'

'No. No, it was just—' Impossible to tell the truth. Jinny said the first thing that came into her head. ' — it was just such an extraordinary name. *Harriet Shakespeare*. I mean, fancy being a writer and being called Shakespeare!'

Both women turned round and stared at her. Mrs Hollins looked scornful and the Hare-woman was obviously amazed. Her mouth opened and her huge eyes grew even wider.

'You haven't heard of Harriet Shakespeare?' she said sharply, as though she thought Jinny was making fun of her.

Damn, thought Jinny. She stuck her chin in the air. 'No I haven't.'

Mrs Hollins saw the chance she had missed earlier and seized it. 'Ah, there's not much Jinny gets to hear about, is there dear?' A sugary smile. 'There's no newspapers or radio or television up at her house. It's all grow your own and make do and mend.'

Why do I not get used to it? thought Jinny despairingly. Every year it happened at least once when the summer visitors were around. Mrs Hollins found a willing ear and showed the Slatterys off to a stranger as though they were creatures in a zoo. Jinny knew the next step from long experience. The stranger would ask interested, over-polite questions, as though Jinny were a freak or an idiot. It shouldn't matter. It was always happening.

Only this time the stranger was the Hare-woman, with her huge, lovely eyes. The eyes which had taken one look at Rachel and understood everything. Jinny could not bear her to get the wrong idea.

'It's quite simple,' she said quickly. 'Nothing peculiar about it. My father's a jeweller — a craftsman — and he's not *forced* to live in a big town to do his job. So we live here, on our own land, and try not to rely on anyone else. Nothing wrong with that, is there?'

The Hare-woman looked at her hard. 'It must make you — a very *close* family,' she said, in a queer voice. 'Not what I'd choose.' Then, as if she sensed Jinny's disappointment, she added, 'Nothing wrong in it, though. And nothing wrong in not having heard of Harriet Shakespeare, either. Pretentious liberal snooper.'

'Ah, but — ' Mrs Hollins could not let that one pass. 'You have to sympathize with her now.'

For a moment the Hare-woman hesitated. Then she said carefully, 'Anyone with children can guess how she's feeling.'

'Well, then!' Mrs Hollins picked on what interested her most. 'Got some yourself, have you?'

'Mmm?' The Hare-woman blinked. 'Yes. I've got a son. Almost fourteen.'

'Fourteen!' said Mrs Hollins brightly. 'Just Rachel's age. And you're staying hereabouts?'

Jinny realized, to her surprise, that she wanted to hear the answer too. She turned away and pretended not to be listening as the woman gave a loud snort of laughter.

'Well, that's what I've come for! You *are* Mrs Hollins, aren't you? We're in your cottage. We finally got here.'

'What? Oh, you're Mrs *Doyle!*' Mrs Hollins was round the counter again in a flash, her hand held out. 'There, and I never thought! Found the key all right, did you? Like I said?'

For a moment, Jinny was bewildered. Then it came to her. They were talking about Back Clough Dale Cottage, and the Hare-woman was one of the people who had come in the middle of the night. Who had made the strange hammering noise.

' — and fancy you having a lad the same age as our Rachel!' Mrs Hollins was saying. 'And there's Keith, too, only four years older. Maybe they'd like to get together.

That's what the young people want. Not too much of the old fogeys.'

Jinny had to look away to stop herself laughing. Could anyone be less like an old fogey than the Hare-woman?

'Philip won't be around much, I'm afraid,' the woman said quickly. 'He's not too well.'

'Ah.' Mrs Hollins pulled a sympathetic face. 'Is it this summer flu that's going round?'

'No. Nothing like that.' Mrs Doyle hesitated. 'He's hurt his head. Just tripped over his own feet and — *wham!*'

'*Just* like our Keith! Boys! The bigger they are the clumsier they get. And untidy! It's like ploughing with dogs to get Keith to clear up after himself.'

You old cow! thought Jinny, because someone had to stick up for Keith. But she did not dare to say it aloud.

The Hare-woman hesitated again. Then she said, 'I thought you'd all be after my blood, as a matter of fact. Because Philip chose the middle of the night to come crashing down. Just as we were arriving here. He made a colossal noise — a great yell and then a thump. We thought he'd woken everyone in the village.'

It was all said quite casually. The kind of thing that people *do* say, half-joking. But it hit Jinny like a fist between the eyes. *It wasn't true.* Nothing like that had happened last night.

But the woman was sounding almost concerned. 'I hope we *didn't* wake you up.'

'Bless you,' Mrs Hollins said. 'There's not a lot of sound comes out of that hollow. You could have murdered your granny down there without anyone hearing.'

The Hare-woman grinned. '*Much* too energetic. We were all on the ropes when we got here. Especially after we'd hauled Philip upstairs. Didn't even have the strength to unpack. We just fell straight into bed.'

Jinny felt as though she had stepped into a midden. *You didn't. You hammered and hammered. On and on and on.* Two lies, then. What was going on?

27

But the woman had begun to hurry, as if she had talked too much. Fishing in the pocket of her jeans, she tugged out a shopping list and started to load herself up with packets and tins and boxes of eggs, cramming them all into a box she had begged. Then she left, without another glance at Jinny. Mrs Hollins looked at her with approval as she strode up the path towards her car.

'There's a nice lady.' She shot a glare at Jinny. 'Pity you couldn't be more polite. Going on about your father! I'd smack Rachel's bottom if she bothered a stranger like that.'

Jinny ignored the scolding and slapped her parcel on to the scales. 'I want to send this first class. Please.'

'Well then, want must be your master.' Triumphantly, Mrs Hollins put the board across the Post Office counter. 'It's nearly half-past one. Think I can stay open whenever I like? There's rules, you know. You'll have to come back this afternoon.'

Why does it matter if she lies?
She's only a stranger.
Just because she saw through Rachel, it doesn't mean she's perfect.

Nagging at herself, Jinny went back along the road and up the track to the farm. But it was no use. She kept seeing those great golden eyes. What was the use of having eyes like that if you did not tell the truth?

With the questions still in her mind, she came into the yard and walked straight across to the outhouse that Joe used as a workshop. Pushing the door open quietly, she stood and watched him for a moment. He was sitting at the bench, intent on a piece of soldering, his long, narrow face peaceful with concentration. Jinny had been trained not to rush in on him, ever since she was a little girl. She waited until his hands stopped moving and he set the work down before she came up to the bench, holding out the parcel.

'Sorry. Mrs Hollins was shut.' She put the parcel on the bench, in an empty space, and went on standing. After a

28

second or two, Joe switched off the soldering iron and put it in its stand, with a sigh.

'O.K. What is it?'

Jinny stared down at the floor, tugging at the sandy plait which hung over her shoulder. 'Suppose — suppose you met someone you liked. Admired a bit, even.' She could feel her face going pink. 'And then, suppose you heard that person tell a lie. Two lies.'

'Yes?' Joe swivelled round on his stool. 'What's the question, then?'

'Well — ' Jinny tugged harder at the plait. 'What would you do? What would you think?'

Joe put his hand under her chin and turned her face until she was looking at him. 'Jinny, you know what I think. Don't fuss about other people and they won't fuss about you. Right? Otherwise—' he grinned '—you'll end up as a worse gossip than Mrs Hollins.'

'But look, let me tell you — '

'No Jin.' He moved his hand over her mouth. 'Whatever it is, I don't want to know. It's not our business. Now how about going in and helping Bella? Mmm? She's drowning in runner beans.'

He turned back to his work and Jinny walked out and across the yard, dragging her feet. He was right, of course. Wasn't he? So — why did she feel as though he was squashing her into a little box? It was in her *nature* to want to know about things. Did that really make her like Mrs Hollins?

When she pushed open the kitchen door, all her questions and protests vanished immediately, swallowed up by chaos. Her mother was sitting at the big, scrubbed, wooden table with a mountain of runner beans in front of her, slicing desperately. And on either side of her was a furious, shouting child.

Oz was tugging at her right arm, putting her in severe danger of cutting herself. 'Mum, I'm *hollow!* I'll never live to be nine if you don't *feed* me! I've got this great pit inside me that's churning and rumbling and—'

On the other side, Louise, the baby, was lying on the floor in a basket, bellowing her head off. As Jinny stepped into the room, Bella put her knife down and yelled.

'*Will* you both stop it, you little monsters! You're driving me off my head!'

At the sound of her voice, Louise screamed even louder, turning purple in the face, and Bella whirled round. Making one of her huge, untidy gestures, she scooped the baby up and hugged her. 'There now! Did your rotten mother bawl at you? You're not a monster at all, are you? You're a dear, lovely little pig-baby.' She rubbed her nose against Louise's cheek. 'And you're starving to death. I'm a horrid, unnatural mother, aren't I? Yes? Yes!'

'*Yes!*' howled Oz.

Jinny stood still taking in the scene, deciding what she should do. Then she stepped forward.

'Honestly, Mum, she'll never shut up unless you feed her. You might as well give in now.'

'But the *beans!*' Bella ran her free hand through her thick, curly hair. 'The beans, the beans, the wretched *beans!* I've got to get this lot done today. There'll be more tomorrow and more the day after that. And if I don't get them done we'll all die of hunger in the winter.'

She pulled a face and let her head lurch dramatically sideways. Oz screeched and tugged at her hair.

'*I* won't starve to death in the winter. I'll have been dead for *months* by then!'

'Waa-aah!' screamed Louise.

Jinny took over. She knew that Bella was really enjoying herself, but the noise was unbearable.

'Look, you feed Louise. I'll give Oz a butty and then *I'll* do the beans.'

'Bless you, you're a dear little freckly angel!' Bella unbuttoned her blouse. 'Bread's in the crock and there's a bit of cheese in the larder.'

Jinny cut a huge doorstep of the heavy wholemeal bread,

smeared it with butter and slammed a lump of crumbly cheese on top. Plugging Oz's mouth with that, she sat down at the table and picked up the knife, beginning to slice the first bean into neat slivers.

'Peace, perfect peace.' Bella smiled sentimentally and ran a finger over Louise's downy head. 'You're a great rescuer, Jin.'

'Have to be, don't I?' Jinny grinned rudely. 'It's a wonder we ever eat at all. This is such a madhouse.'

'Jolly, though.' Bella picked up a raw bean and began to chew it. 'Just think. If we'd stayed in London, we'd be a boring, ordinary family. Probably be driving off with a caravan for our boring holidays in the country. Pretending we knew how people in the country live. At least this is *real*.'

'So that's what real life is like,' Jinny said. 'No money and a mountain of runner beans. I always wondered.'

'Coo, you're ratty.' Bella smiled her big, sleepy smile. 'Been quarrelling with someone? Keith?'

'Not really,' said Jinny. Then she remembered something. 'Mum — '

'Mmm?'

'Who's Harriet Shakespeare?'

Bella munched at her bean. 'What on earth d'you want to know *that* for?'

'Oh nothing. It's just that — someone — laughed at me because I'd not heard of her.'

'Aha! I knew something had bitten you. Well, she's nothing exciting. A tele-lady. Sort of journalist, I suppose. I think she specializes in snooping round peculiar political groups. Finding out scare stories. Just the sort of person Joe can't stand.' She took another enormous bite of her bean. 'How did she come up?'

'Her son,' Jinny said. 'He's being held hostage in London. It was on the radio while I was in the Post Office.'

'*Don't* tell me!' Bella gave a wicked chuckle. 'Mrs Hollins grinned all over her face and said, "There's a terrible thing!" Aren't I right?'

31

But it is terrible, thought Jinny. *For the boy.* Then she remembered something, and she smiled after all. 'You're not quite right. It was worse than that. She said, "Think if it had been our Rachel!"'

'Oh!' said Bella longingly. '*Oh! If only.*' Her eyes met Jinny's and she gave such a loud shriek of laughter that the baby jerked an arm and knocked a landslide of beans on to the floor.

Day Three — Tuesday 9th August

8.00 a.m.

Tug crouched on his bed, watching the door. Waiting. He had not slept since the Man and the Woman walked out, after that first visit, hours ago. The noise and the fear, jangling together in his head, made it impossible to relax and he had no idea what time it was. He knew there had been a night, because all through it he had watched the dark skylight, spattered with stars, but his watch said eleven o'clock on the fourth of March and he was certain it was wrong. Or almost certain.

He was very hungry and thirsty, but he had not even touched the water in the plastic jug. He had just stayed on his bed, alert and tense, waiting for Them to come back. Fighting his headache and the monotonous, obsessive beat of the band while he tried to *think*. Now all his questions were ready and his eyes were fixed on the latch.

When it finally moved, it was almost an anti-climax. The Man let himself in, with a louder burst of sound as the door opened.

. . . the KEEL row . . . .

Walking over to the bed, he looked Tug up and down, taking his time. Somehow it was impossible to speak first.

'Sleep well?' he said at last.

'No.' Tug's voice came out as a croak from a dry, sore throat.

'Have some water.' The Man nodded at the jug. Seeing

33

Tug's hesitation, he grinned slowly. 'It won't poison you.' He crossed to the chest of drawers, picked up the jug and drank from it. Then he held it out.

I'm not taking anything from you, Tug wanted to say. *Not until you tell me what's going on.* Only — the dryness in his throat was almost unbearable and he did not see how there *could* be anything wrong with the water.

The Man shrugged.

Sliding off the bed, Tug padded across the floor and took the jug. He did not put it down until it was almost empty. Then he said, 'Don't you think it's time you — '

'Sit down on the bed,' said the Man.

'But I don't want — ' began Tug.

Then he saw, from the Man's faint frown, that he was being unwise. He went over to the bed and sat on it. When he was safely there, the Man opened the door, stepped through it and bent down, still watching Tug over his shoulder. It was impossible to see what he was doing, but his hand reached out along the floor outside.

And suddenly the music stopped.

The relief was so enormous that Tug's ears tingled with it and he flopped back against the wall as though his muscles had been disconnected. Beautiful, magic silence. It was not spoilt, even by the smile on the Man's face which showed that he perfectly understood the lightness, the freedom from struggling against the noise.

Then, in the quiet, another pair of feet began to climb the stairs. Slowly and carefully, each clack of a heel sounding extraordinarily loud. Tug leaned forward as the door opened wider and the Woman walked in with a tray. She stood for a moment, letting him see what was on it.

'Breakfast,' she said.

It was a dream breakfast. Bacon and egg and sausage and beans and tomatoes. All steaming hot. A rack of toast with marmalade and butter in dishes. And a big mug of tea. Tug had never realized before that people's mouths really watered. Now it was all he could do not to dribble. He stared at the tray, and the Woman went on standing by the door holding it.

'Well?' he said at last. 'Isn't it for me?'

She nodded. 'Oh yes, it's for you all right.'

'Do you want me to come and fetch it?'

'No. I'll give it to you. But what do you say, first?'

As if I was a snotty little kid, thought Tug in disgust. It seemed ridiculous. But — what did it matter?

'Thank you,' he said.

'Thank you — ' she left the words hanging and raised her eyebrows.

Guessing games? When he was starving? Perhaps it was a sort of torture. Bewildered, Tug looked from one to the other. 'I don't get it. Thank you — what?'

'You usually call her something,' said the Man. Softly and dangerously.

An idea of what they wanted began to seep into Tug's head. And yet — were they *serious?* In spite of the colour of his hair, in spite of the madness of everything, he had not quite been able to believe it. And even now he played ignorant.

'I don't know what you're talking about. *What* do I usually call her?'

It was the Woman who answered. 'Ma,' she said. 'You call me Ma.'

It caught him off balance. He had been bracing himself for her to say 'Mum', ready to mock at it in his head because she didn't look like anyone's Mum. But — Ma? He looked at her as she stood there, alert and threatening, poised on the balls of her feet. Ma? Perhaps.

'Your breakfast's getting cold,' she said, watching him. But he was not ready to give in yet. He turned to stare at the Man.

'And I suppose I call you Pa,' he muttered. Rudely. Disbelievingly.

The Man smiled calmly, as though he had been waiting for just that question. 'No. You could, but you don't. You call me Doyle.'

35

Doyle . . . Ma . . . Tug's eyes flickered from one to the other. It was complicated. It almost had the gritty feel of truth. Suddenly he bunched his fists and screwed his eyes up. 'You're both *mad!*' he shouted. 'You're mad, you're mad! You can't really expect me to believe this rubbish! Why don't you tell me what's going on and — '

The door crashed shut. He opened his eyes again and saw that the Woman had walked out, taking his breakfast with her.

'Stupid,' said Doyle softly. 'You've upset her.'

'But — ' Tug stammered, and then stopped. They couldn't be going to starve him to death. Not just for that. Could they?

'Funny how strange mothers are.' Doyle's voice was as light as a thought. He tilted his head towards the door and Tug heard the sound of footsteps coming up the stairs again. 'I shouldn't risk another upset,' Doyle murmured.

Tug heard the Woman climbing, slowly and carefully. Carrying a tray. Eerily, as though he were watching a replay of his life, he saw the door open. She stepped inside and stood still.

The food looked just as hot and delicious as it had before. Tug could smell it from where he was sitting.

'Breakfast,' said the Woman.

Tug looked sideways at Doyle, but Doyle did not speak. Then he looked towards the food on the tray and thought. He did not understand why they were playing this charade, but playing charades would not kill him. Not like starvation. And what did a word matter? He did not even use that word for his mother.

He took a deep breath.

'Thank you — Ma.'

The Woman did not smile or look triumphant. She simply stepped across the room, laid the tray on his lap and walked back to the door. And Tug felt as though something had drained out of him, leaving him small and empty.

Doyle stepped after her on to the landing, but when he was

outside, he turned and smiled slowly, looking straight into Tug's eyes.

'Have a good breakfast — Philip.'

'I'm *not* Philip,' Tug yelled. 'And you're *not* my parents!'

But the door had already closed. Feeling sick, Tug pushed the tray off his lap and walked over to the wardrobe. Opening it, he stared into the mirror and the hateful, strange face with the black hair stared back at him. But it was not as strange as it had been the first time he saw it. Somehow, in the time in between, his brain had adjusted and now when he looked at it he saw his own face at once.

His first, angry urge was to smash the glass. To beat at it with his fist until the face was smashed into thousands of pieces. But the first thump had no effect at all and, losing heart, he changed his mind. He leaned forward and began to breathe on the glass. The face disappeared in a misty blur and Tug wrote across it, scrawling the capitals with his forefinger.

I'M NOT PHILIP

I'M TUG

But even before he had finished, the mist evaporated and the letters vanished, leaving the black-haired face staring angrily back at him.

And then the music started again. It was a double torture, taking his mind off guard and shattering the precious silence.

10.00 a.m.

Forget it, Jinny told herself. *It's not our business. Like Dad said. Forget it. Forget it.*

She jabbed with her hoe at the ground between the cabbages. Half her mind was busy watching the blade shuffle through the dry, stony earth, avoiding the cabbage stalks and noticing what a mess the slugs and caterpillars had made. But the other half was distracted, seeing the Hare-woman's face against the background of green, purple-tinged leaves. That long, strong face with the golden, hunted eyes. Telling lies.

Oh, rot it. *Rot* it! She jabbed harder and unwisely with the hoe and it sliced through the last cabbage stalk. The plant flopped over sideways and Jinny sighed as she bent down to pick it up. It was no use pretending. She could not concentrate on what she was doing. *Why* had the Hare-woman lied about the noises in the night? What had the hammering been for? What had been going on in Mrs Hollins's cottage while the hare was running through the field, towards the net?

There's no connection, she said to herself severely. *Just that you feel guilty.* Oh, very clever, Jinny Slattery. Full marks for brilliant psychology. Only — how did that help? She still felt the same. Some part of her was desperate to understand the mystery and to know why the strong, beautiful Hare-woman had the eyes of a fugitive. Back Clough Dale Cottage still crouched at the edges of her mind, dark and mysterious, drawing her towards it.

Well, it would be better to go there and get it over than to spend all day mooching about! She made the decision quite suddenly, without a struggle. It meant sneaking off, of course. When she had finished the hoeing, she should have gone into the kitchen to help Bella with the next lot of beans. Only after that it would be lunch and then Joe would take her up to Long Piece to start lifting the old broad bean plants. Before she knew where she was, it would be time to shut the hens up and get on with the evening milking. For the first time she could remember, she felt resentful. If Rachel Hollins could spend the whole summer sunning herself on the wall showing off her new dresses, why couldn't Jinny Slattery take half an hour off? She would!

Even then, she did not just drop the hoe and leave. Quite automatically, she carried it back to the tool-house, lobbing the broken cabbage into the pigsty as she went. She did not go until she had cleaned the blade of the hoe and hung it up in its proper place, as Joe had taught her to when she was five years old.

When she went, she slid quietly across the yard, trying to avoid disturbing the chickens. Ferry was lying stretched in the sun at the start of the track and he raised his head and pricked his ears as her shadow fell across him.

'Ssss . . . .' hissed Jinny softly. 'I'm truanting. Don't give me away.'

He lowered his head again and she slipped out of the yard and off down to the road. With every step she took, she felt sillier and sillier. She had no plan, no idea of what she expected to happen. Just an urge to go to the cottage and hang around outside. She loitered along the road and by the time she reached the track that led into Back Clough Dale she was almost ready to turn round and go home after all.

Then, behind her, she heard the sound of a car. She squashed herself up against the wall, just in time, as an old white Ford Escort turned on to the track. The Hare-woman was at the wheel. She wore a shabby, checked shirt with the sleeves rolled up and she was driving with the window open and one elbow on the ledge.

Jinny gulped stupidly. By the time she had pulled herself together enough to wave and smile, the car was topping the crest of the path. The next moment it had dropped down into the hollow beyond, out of sight.

Rot it, thought Jinny. Why was she always so slow? If only she had reacted faster, she could have spoken . . . . In her mind, she ran the scene over again:

Jinny: (brightly, as the car slowed to turn the corner) Hallo! Mrs Doyle, isn't it?
Hare-woman: (pleased to be remembered) That's right.
Jinny: How's your son? I thought you said he'd banged his head.
Hare-woman: Oh, he's much better now. In fact, I think he'd like a visitor. Why don't you . . . .

(No. Scrub that last bit. She thought of something better.)

39

Harewoman: (biting her lip) Well, he didn't exactly . . . .
(stares into Jinny's eyes) Look, I get the feeling that you
understand things. I couldn't explain it to everyone, but I'd
like to tell you. Why don't you jump into the car and . . . .

Oh rot it, *that* was no use. Real life simply wasn't like that.
And anyway, try as she might, Jinny could not think of a
single sensible answer to all the questions in her mind. She
frowned and plodded on up the track until she reached the
gate that she and Joe had netted. From there she could see the
roof of the cottage. If she went on any further, the people in
the cottage would be able to see her, and there was no chance
of pretending that she was just passing. The track did not go
anywhere else.

But there were other ways of getting close to the cottage.
She opened the gate and slipped into the field that had been
the hare's field. If she squeezed through the stile on the left,
she would come out on to the scrubby wooded slope that ran
round the top of the dale, below the open moor. And under
cover of the trees she could work her way round until she was
looking down into the hollow from behind the cottage.

The stile was jammed, choked with the gorse branches
that Joe had squashed into the gap to prevent the hare's
escape. *Careless*, Jinny thought. It would not have been good
if those tell-tale branches had been discovered by someone
with an eye for poachers. She would have to tell Joe . . . .

Then she remembered that she could not possibly tell,
because he would be horrified if he knew where she had been
and why. Gritting her teeth against the prickles, she pushed
the branches through and then squeezed through the stile
herself, into the wood. Dry leaves rustled under her feet as
she walked and she peered around, noticing things. The
bilberries on the scattered bushes were almost ripe. Probably
meant they were quite ready up on the moor. And there was a
good crop of blackberries coming. One or two chanterelles,
as well, with their inside-out yellow mushroom heads.

It was second nature to her to notice things like that,

whatever she was doing, because that was how Joe had brought her up. She sometimes thought that if he went to a garden party at Buckingham Palace he would spend the time searching for dandelion leaves to put in his salads. But it did not make her forget why she had come. She padded carefully round the curve of the slope, holding on to tree-trunks to brace herself against the steepness of the ground, until she could stand gazing down into the hollow, screened by the trees.

There was not much to see. No people sitting out in the sun. No washing hanging to dry in the tiny metre of garden behind the cottage. The only sign of life was the noise of a radio being played somewhere inside. *Brass band music*, thought Jinny absently, as she stared down at the grim, grey building, squatting sharp-cornered and dour in its private dent in the dale.

And yet — there was something different about the cottage. Something that Jinny could not quite put her finger on. She went a few steps nearer, down the slope, holding on to a hazel bush to stop herself sliding. What *was* it? There was something unfamiliar about the roof. Up where the skylight cut into the grey stone tiles . . . .

She leaned slightly sideways, holding tightly to the branch, and suddenly a voice spoke from below.

'Hallo.'

It was not loud, but it startled her and she jerked. The hazel branch broke and, robbed of its support she started to slither. Reaching out to catch at another bush, she lost her footing and tumbled head over heels, scratching her arms and bumping her back, until she landed at the bottom of the slope, hard up against the wooden rails of the garden.

'That was very dramatic,' said the voice.

Jinny looked up. It was not the Hare-woman. It was a man with very dark hair and very pale blue eyes that were staring disturbingly at her. She started to speak, babbling uncontrollably.

'Look, I'm sorry, I'd not meant to disturb you. It was just

41

that I could not stop myself falling — '

Shock, said the practical part of her brain. *You're shocked.* But knowing that did not help her to deal with it. The words went on flooding out of her.

' — only you startled me and I lost my footing and I was just — '

'Practising skiing?' said the man. But somehow it was not a joke. He had broken in to stop her talking. And he was still staring. Jinny clutched at the first explanation that came into her head, before he could begin to ask her questions.

'Oh no, not skiing. No, it was — puff-balls.'

'Puff-balls?' The man did not allow that to be a joke either. He raised very black eyebrows above his pale eyes and waited for an explanation.

'Yes — you know.' Jinny sketched a huge circle in the air. 'Fungi. Giant puff-balls. Sometimes you can find them in the wood up there'. The music from the house suddenly grew louder and she raised her voice automatically. 'They're fantastic if you slice them up and fry them with bacon — '

'Delicious.' The cold voice cut her off short. Reaching over the fence, the man gripped her shoulder and pulled her to her feet, his fingers digging in roughly. 'If I see any, I'll let you know. Until then, perhaps you'd like to do your mushroom hunting somewhere else. We're here on holiday. For a rest. We can do without people crashing in through the kitchen window.'

He did not frown or raise his voice, but his whole way of speaking was so unpleasant that Jinny shuddered. And all the time he was talking he was edging her round the side of the cottage, still holding on to her shoulder across the fence. They were almost at the front when, without any warning, the music blared suddenly, ten times louder, from up by the roof. Above it, even louder yet, a voice shrilled in a single, desperate shout. Then there was a thud and the music softened again.

The man's fingers tightened sharply, digging into Jinny as she turned towards the shout. Had she really heard — what

42

she thought she had heard? She repeated the sound in her head, trying to work out something else that it could have been and listening for more.

But the only noise that came from the house was the muffled, repetitive music. And the man beside her threw his head back and shouted, 'Oh, give it a break, Philip. We've got visitors. If you fool around like that we'll land up with the N.S.P.C.C. on our doorstep.'

It was casual — the shout of a parent who knows that he should go and scold a child, but who can't be bothered. A perfect performance. It would have convinced Jinny completely, except that she had felt his fingers on her shoulder when he first heard the shout. There had been something fierce about that startled tightening that did not go with the lazy, good-natured shout. It went with the cold eyes and the unfriendly way that he had been speaking to her.

Go, said her mind, sensing things that it could not understand. *Get out of here.* But she was still shocked and shaking from her fall and she could not work out how to slide off calmly and politely. She felt that she needed to say something else.

'I hope he's not really hurt,' she said. 'He sounded quite scared. For a boy of fourteen.' As soon as the words were out, they sounded wrong. Rude and interfering.

The man obviously thought so too. His lips narrowed. 'You'd like to come and check, would you?' he said nastily.

For one, wild second, Jinny wondered whether she should say 'Yes'. Because, after all, there *had* been a shout. A frightened, worrying shout. Could you just ignore something like that?

Then the Slattery part of her mind took over, and she realized how stupid she was being. Fancy thinking of poking round in other people's affairs, for no real reason!

While she was hesitating, the man made it impossible for her to reply. He looked her up and down with an offensive, patronizing smile. 'Well, of course you can come in, if you really want to look Philip over. But I'm afraid you'd be

43

disappointed. He's very uninterested in girls. For a boy of fourteen.'

Jinny went pink, all in a rush, and backed away. 'I can't—' she said hastily. 'I—that is—I've got to go home.'

Then she turned and walked away, feeling as though her feet were enormous. It took all her energy not to burst into tears and run, but she clenched her teeth and made herself move slowly. All the time that horrible man could see her. He had made her feel beastly. Cringing and simpering and coy and — like *Rachel*.

Every step seemed to take twenty minutes. She was certain that the man was standing watching, sneering at her. And all the time she could hear her stupid, squeaky voice saying, *He sounded quite scared. For a boy of fourteen . . . a boy of fourteen . . . a boy of fourteen . . . .*

As soon as she was sure that she was over the rise and he could not see her, she started to race, screwing up her fists and biting her lip so that she did not collapse into tears. She was muddled and shaken and upset. She had to talk to someone sensible who would not laugh or be angry with her. Someone who would listen properly.

She had to talk to Keith.

10.30 a.m.

When Tug finally finished his cold, congealed breakfast, he did not feel like doing anything at all. Just lying stretched out on the bed, trying to forget where he was and what he looked like and what had happened. Giving himself up to the tune that seemed to have woven itself into his body, so that his heart and his pulse must surely beat in time to 'The Keel Row'. So that the words filled his brain, continually repeated, and he breathed through Sandgate.

But Hank's voice cut into the rhythms, disturbing his stupor. He knew exactly what she would say:

There you go again! (Standing over him with her fists clenched.) *Slumping like a wet jelly! I spend my whole life fighting and struggling and taking risks. How did I ever come to have a son like you, with no fight in him?*

'It's all right for you,' he said out loud. 'Fighting bombers and terrorists and things — that's your job and you like it. You like it so much that you can't even stay at home long enough to wash my socks!'

That made him feel better, in a queer way. Almost normal. He quite often started the morning by having a shouting match with Hank. It got his adrenalin flowing before he did his exercises.

Once he had thought that, it seemed natural to carry on with the routine as far as he could. Slipping off the bed, he did a few loosening-up exercises, swinging from the waist with his arms outstretched, and reaching for the ground.

It was impossible to break into the music and set up a new beat of his own, so he swung and stretched in time to it, feeling ridiculously like a fat woman in a keep-fit class.

>   . . . *Weel* may the *keel* row
>   That *my laddie's in.*
>   As *I* came through *Sand*gate . . . .

Round and back. Round and back. Round and back. Bend. Bend. Bend. Bend. Bend.

It was hypnotic. Now not only his mind but his body had joined in with the steady thud that filled the room. The thud went on and on, constantly, without altering speed, and Tug could not alter his speed either. Nor could he stop. He went on with the same easy, loosening exercises, minute after minute, mechanically.

The regular movement had almost worked him into a trance when he heard the noises from outside — a slither, a crash and a shout, faint and nearly blotted out by the music. His first feeling was irritation. The noises weren't regular. They didn't fit his rhythm. Something was going on outside that interfered with his thudding, swinging, stretching concentration.

His mind jerked back to normal. *Something was going on outside!* Clambering on to the bed, he reached through the grid and pushed the skylight open a crack. Fresh air flowed in, as invigorating as cold water and, carried on it, came a girl's voice saying ' — they're fantastic if you slice them up and fry them with bacon.'

A strange girl's voice.

The shock of realization broke the last shreds of the music's mesmerizing spell. He strained his ears to catch the girl's voice again, to see if he could work out whether she was one of Them.

But she did not speak again. Instead, Tug heard Doyle's voice, too low for him to make out the words. He bit his thumb-nail. Was it worth the risk of trying to do something, or would that only put him in more danger?

Then he heard feet on the stairs, coming up fast. Running. It was now or never, and how could he miss the only chance he had had so far? Pushing the skylight as wide open as possible, he pressed his open mouth up close to the grid and yelled as the door was flung open.

'*Help!*'

The next moment, the Woman had smashed into him, her whole weight thudding against his legs. He went straight down and hit his head on the wall before he rolled from the bed to the floor. She pinned him there, with one knee on his chest and one strong hand over his mouth and nose, so that he could hardly breathe. The other hand was curved like a claw, the fingers splayed out just above Tug's eyes, ready to jab.

'Don't think I wouldn't!' she hissed. 'I know what I'm doing. I've been trained.'

Her voice shook and the hand over Tug's face was trembling slightly, but she did not alter her position. Dimly, behind the threatening fingers, he could see her face, sharp with concentration, watching his and trying to hear what was going on outside. But nothing was audible above the music until, after some time, the front door downstairs slammed.

'*Right!*' the Woman said. 'Now you learn to do what you're told.'

She hit him hard across the face with the flat of her hand. The blow caught his cheek-bone and his ear, jarring his jaw.

'Understand?'

She hit him again, on the other side of his face. When he opened his mouth to say that she was hurting him, she hit him across the mouth, making him bite his tongue. And again. And again. And again.

The first three blows were so painful that Tug could not think of anything except how much they hurt. But as his face grew slightly numb, he began to feel something else. A terrible feeling that she would never stop. That now she had started she did not know any way of stopping herself. She too had fallen into the rhythm of the never-ending tune, so that the blows fell with the beat.

Weel . . . keel . . .
. . . keel . . . keel . . . .

On and on, so that it seemed she would never end, like the tune, but go on for ever, while Tug gritted his teeth, struggling not to scream, *not* to scream, because when he started he would be like her and go on and on and on and on —

And then, suddenly, Doyle was there. Out of nowhere, it seemed, he appeared behind the Woman and laid a single finger on her shoulder. Just one finger. And no words. But it was enough. She stood up, panting slightly, and stared down at Tug.

'Stupid cow,' said Doyle calmly. 'Should have left his *face* alone. Go and get some ice-cubes and stuff.'

She vanished at once. Doyle went on staring down with no expression.

'She hit me,' Tug said weakly, appealing for sympathy. 'Just because I — '

Doyle shrugged. 'You have to understand,' he said quietly. 'We'll kill you if we need to.'

It was a moment of total stillness that even made the brass band fade into the background. He stood looking down at Tug and Tug looked back, thinking that he had never been truly afraid before. It was not the sort of physical panic that makes people wet themselves. It was something much colder and stronger and deeper, like a scar across his brain. For the first time in his life, he understood that he might die. Not in a hundred years, or when he was very old, but now. Today or tomorrow. In this room.

And yet — the moment passed. Not two minutes later, Doyle and the Woman were kneeling on either side of him, attending to his face like anxious, careful parents. The Woman cleared away the dried clots which had bled from his nose and once or twice she touched a bruise roughly and he winced. But Doyle was as deft and professional as a nurse, holding ice-cubes to Tug's swollen mouth and to the lump on his head where he had hit the wall.

It was a long time before they were satisfied. The Woman stopped first. Sitting back on her heels, she studied Tug's face carefully.

'Not a pretty sight. But no worse than usual.'

He scowled at her.

'Pack it in.' She tweaked his hair, almost gently.

Doyle jerked his head. 'You're O.K. now. On the bed.'

Automatically, Tug obeyed, clambering up and stretching out full length. They did not need to make any threats as they left him. The threat hung in the air, keeping him motionless on the bed, even when there was no one to watch him.

I could die.

Apathy dropped over him like a blanket. Nothing stirred it, not even the thought of Hank. Oh, she would certainly yell at him if she could see him now, but he would not have the energy to shout back. He could not even be bothered to work out what she would say. She seemed very distant and insubstantial.

I could die.

He lay staring at the ceiling until the door opened again and Doyle came in, carrying a chair and a large shoulder-bag. He placed the chair directly in front of the door and sat on it, stretching his legs.

'We've decided that you need company,' he said coolly.

So they were going to watch him now, were they? Tug did not even have the strength to resent it. He lay on the bed gazing listlessly at Doyle.

Keeping his eyes on Tug, Doyle reached down for the shoulder-bag, unzipped it and pulled out a rag. His mouth moved as though something amused him, but he did not speak. From where he was sitting, he would have had to shout to make himself heard.

Then he took out something else. Something that was a dull, dark grey, with a heavy, ribbed handle and a narrow, cylindrical barrel. Carefully he began to rub at one side of it, peering critically at the surface and holding it up to the light from time to time. Tug knew that the whole thing was being done for him to watch. So that he knew. He lay quite still and silent, unable to stop looking at the gun.

Eventually Doyle glanced up and smiled slowly. Raising a hand, he beckoned, still without speaking. As if he had been mesmerized, Tug swung his legs off the bed and walked across the room. When he reached the chair, Doyle caught hold of his hand and raised it, laying the fingers against the barrel of the gun, so that Tug could feel the cold metal. Then he smiled again.

'Nice little thing, isn't it?' He weighed the gun in his hand. 'P38. A bit long, but nice and light. It weighs more with the magazine in, of course.'

'Magazine?' Tug said stupidly.

'To load it.' Doyle felt in the bag again, took out something and slid it into the handle of the gun. 'See? Now it's ready to fire. But you can't have forgotten all that. Not after all the years you've helped me with my guns.'

'Helped?' Tug said, bewildered. It was hard to pay attention to the words, while Doyle watched him with glittering eyes and the muzzle of the loaded gun pointed towards him. 'Helped with guns?'

'My hobby,' Doyle said softly. 'Facsimile guns. Copies. The sort of hobby lots of fathers have. Mmm?'

Tug gazed at the muzzle of the gun and swallowed, with a dry throat.

'Funny,' murmured Doyle, his finger on the trigger. 'If you didn't *know* it was a fake, you'd never guess, would you? It looks quite — real.'

Tug was ready to dissolve with terror. The narrow barrel of the gun pointed at him like a skeleton finger. He did not believe for a moment that it was a fake. He just kept thinking, *Suppose his finger jerks by accident. Suppose . . . .*

Then Doyle laughed. Spinning the gun round on his finger, he slid the magazine out and dropped it back into the bag. Then he started to rub at the metal again. 'It wouldn't frighten you, of course,' he said casually. 'You're too used to handling the guns. It's nice to have a son who shares my interests.'

Now that the threat was removed, Tug was suddenly savagely angry. 'You're not still pretending, are you?' His rage nearly choked him. 'Not after what that woman did to me? You can't still be pretending that you're my parents.'

'Where do you think most murders happen?' murmured Doyle. 'And baby-batterings and granny-bashings and wife-beatings?'

'But — '

'Who do you think the best torturers are?' Doyle went on, without letting Tug speak. 'Your nearest and dearest, of course. They're the ones you can't leave easily. You care about what they think. And they know where your weak places are. Husbands and wives are bad enough. But mothers and fathers are the worst. You can never get rid of them. They have you when you're young and weak and they've got you for ever.'

It was all said quite mildly, without any venom, while he went on rubbing the gun.

'Then why are you treating me like this?' Tug said quickly. 'If you can see all that, why are you still so cruel to me?'

'Cruel?' Doyle raised his eyebrows. 'We're not *cruel* to you, Philip. We're doing our best by you. But we're prisoners of the family ourselves. Just like everyone else.'

And he held the gun up to the light again, whistling through his teeth.

11.00 a.m.

Jinny was still running when she reached the edge of the village. She had to make herself stop so that she had a chance to get her breath back. It would be asking for trouble to arrive panting and upset if Rachel happened to be about.

But as she came up to the Post Office, she could see that it was all right. Rachel was busy. She was sitting on her wall again, but so were David and Harry Tansley and Andrew Walsh. All vying with each other to make clever comments and impress her. Rachel was being sweet and feminine, smiling at all of them and laughing at one joke in five. She barely looked as Jinny scuttled past towards the back door.

There was not even any need to knock. As she reached it, Mr Hollins came out, putting on his helmet. He gave her a strange glance, but he did not comment. Just pushed the door wider.

'Go on in, lass. Keith's in the lounge. *If* you can see him under all his muddle. See if you can get him to tidy up a bit before his Mam — *you* know.'

Jinny nodded. 'Yes. Thanks.' Her voice sounded squeaky

and odd to her, but Mr Hollins did not seem to notice. He walked away and she made for the lounge door.

'*Keith!*'

He was sitting at the table with a huge heap of newspapers in front of him and more on the floor. Jinny was so relieved to see his heavy, solemn face that she launched herself forward.

'I've got to tell you, only it's so difficult to explain when I — oh Keith, it was *awful!*'

Once she started speaking, she began to cry, and her nose and her eyes streamed as her voice babbled on and on.

' — he was horrible and really I'd not done a thing to set him off, but he made me feel — '

Keith was not in the least put out. He coped with her, just as he had been coping ever since he was ten and she was a scared five year old, being bullied by the other children at school because of her southern accent. He stood up and let her crash against him, putting an arm round her while she wailed into the front of his jumper.

When he had given her a couple of minutes to get over the worst of it, he said, 'Tea.'

'Oh, you're right, and I'm sorry to come yelling in here, but it's shock I'm sure and — '

'Of course it's shock,' Keith said calmly. 'The whole side of your face is a right mess. What have you been up to?'

Jinny lifted a hand and touched her cheek. It was sore in some places and numb in others and her fingers came away with blood on them. 'I fell. Down the slope in Back Clough Dale. And then a man came and he said — he said — '

Keith pushed her down into a chair. 'It's soft to try and talk before you're over the shock. Here, drink this and wait till you're calmed down.'

He thrust his own mug of tea into her hand. Jinny pulled a face at the sweetness, but after a sip or two she felt less shaky. she reached out to put the mug down, but there was no space. The open newspapers covered every inch of the table. Automatically, she started to push them into a pile.

'You are a *slob*, Keith. You know your Mam'll go mad if

she sees this lot. How anyone can be as clever as you and not
learn — '

'Glad you're better.' Keith grinned at her and pulled away
a copy of the *Sun*. 'Now let my work alone and tell us what's
up.'

'It's — ' Jinny felt her throat begin to tighten as she
thought about what had happened. All at once, she was not
so sure that she did want to talk about it. It would sound so
thin. She turned back to the papers. 'Work? How's reading
the papers *work?*'

'Tell you after.' Firmly, Keith took her hands away from
The Times and the *Daily Express* and the *Guardian*. 'When
you've pulled your head out of the sand. What is it, now? Tell
Uncle Keith. Cow got foot and mouth? Handsome stranger
passed by and broken your heart?'

Jinny smiled.

'Aha! It *is* the handsome stranger!'

''Course it's not. Why not listen if you're that keen to
hear?'

Keith looked exaggeratedly solemn. 'My ears are flapping.'
Putting his hands up on either side of his head, he waggled
them.

'No, *really* listen.' Jinny twisted her hands together in her
lap and stared down at them, working out where to start.
Setting everything in order in her head. She began with
hearing the people arrive at the cottage in the middle of the
night. But she left out her reason for being out so late. It was
not fair to tell Keith things like that, not with his father being
a policeman. He noticed the gap, of course, and she saw him
blink, but he did not say anything.

'Then yesterday morning I met the woman. In the shop.
She — ' Jinny hesitated. But there was no point in trying to
explain what the Hare-woman was like. Better to stick to
facts. 'She told two lies. Said that her son had a noisy fall
when they came. Noisy enough to waken the village. And
that they went straight to bed after. But it wasn't like that.
None of it.'

Keith nodded. 'And Mam said about the hollow shutting the noise in?'

'Yes,' said Jinny eagerly. 'Do you think the woman was checking if anyone heard the hammering?'

'Hmm. Don't know yet. Carry on a bit. There must have been something today, to set you in such a state.'

'Today.' Jinny felt herself grow pink. 'Yes, today I went up round Back Clough Dale.'

'You did?' Keith looked at her as though he were amused. 'And what was that for, then?'

Jinny went pinker still. 'Well, I thought I'd take a look. Because it was queer.'

'I see,' Keith said gravely. 'And you slipped down the slope? Behind the cottage?'

'Yes. There was a man came out. He shouted and then he was horrible, trying to get me away.' She slipped quickly over that bit. There was no call to tell Keith what the man had said. 'But that's not it. The thing is — what I heard. While he was sending me off.'

'So? Tell us quick, or I'll die of excitement.'

Jinny slapped his hand. 'It's *serious*.'

''Course it is. Go on, then.'

'*I heard someone shouting "Help!"*'

'Ah.' Keith nodded slowly.

'I *did*,' said Jinny fiercely. 'It was very loud. There was some music or something, but I still heard it, even over that noise. The person who shouted *meant* it.'

'And the man? What did he do?'

'Oh, nothing much. Said it was his son playing games. But I'm sure — Oh, come on Keith. Stop larking about and tell me what you think.'

'What I think?' Keith stopped laughing and looked at her almost gently. 'I think it's the handsome stranger after all.'

'W — what do you mean?' said Jinny. Stammering, because she knew really.

'This woman that you met. What's she like? A bit special?'

'That's nothing to do with it!' Jinny said sharply. 'Nothing at all. I've been telling you facts. About the hammering and the lies, and the voice shouting for help. *That's* what I want your opinion of.'

'What's a *fact*? Facts depend on how you look at them.' Keith waved a hand at the newspapers, upsetting Jinny's neat pile. '*These* have all got the same facts, more or less. But they make different stories out of them, to suit their own interests. That's why I've got them. It's my Media Studies project for the summer — to take a particular story and follow it through all the papers for a week, to see what different things they all make of the same *facts*. And you're the same. You've made a big mystery out of a few little scraps. Because you're interested in this woman. You feel she *should* have a story round her.'

'But what about the voice that shouted "Help"?' Jinny said stubbornly. Why was Keith being so stupid? 'I can't ignore *that*, can I?'

'Oh, come *on!*' Keith shook his head at her. 'You're so *earnest*, Jin. That's the trouble with all you Slatterys. No idea of fun. Look, when I was eight, I sat up in the dark, flashing SOS with my torch. And half the village came knocking at the back door, in a panic.'

'But — '

'But *nothing*.' He ran a hand through his thick, dark hair, so that it stood on end even more than before. 'Listen to me, you stupid freckled peasant. Yes. *Yes*. I do think it's a touch odd, your story. Just a touch, mind. But what can I do? Get Dad to go down and play the heavy policeman? He'd laugh me out of the village if I suggested it. *He's* not forgotten that SOS, either.'

'So — what do I do?' Jinny banged her fist on the table, and Keith grinned.

'Always have to be *doing*, don't you? Well, there's nothing you can do, unless you can find another *fact* or two. Do that, and I'll get my Dad out. If you can make it sound good.'

'But you'll not help me?' Jinny stood up.

'I've got to *work*, haven't I? Got to read all these newspapers.' He waved his hand at them again and even more slid on to the floor. 'I've not even chosen the story I'm going to do. Hey!' He looked up at her with studied innocence. 'You could stay and help me. Have a look through the papers and choose a good subject.'

I know what you're up to, thought Jinny. He was trying to distract her. To make her forget the Hare-woman and the strange happenings in Back Clough Dale. But she was not going to be distracted. She made for the door. 'No chance. I have to go home and slice beans.'

Keith shrugged. 'Oh well, I suppose there's no use in telling you to think about it while you slice. You don't know what's in the news, do you.' He raised his eyebrows, pulling a comic, despairing face.

'Yes I do!' Jinny said triumphantly. She remembered the Hare-woman standing in the Post Office, straining her ears to listen to the radio. 'Why don't you do Harriet Shakespeare's son? Being held a hostage?' It amused her to suggest that. When Keith had started talking about the project just to turn her mind from the Hare-woman. 'Yes, I think that's what you ought to do.'

'Mmm.' Keith stopped pulling faces and looked thoughtful. 'Not bad. A bit obvious, but there'll be lots of coverage. And it'd be good to see which papers go for the human interest — the sob stuff — and which ones go into the terrorists' reasons properly. Terrorists always have such complicated reasons. Why don't you stay and help me — ?'

'Beans!' Jinny said firmly as she ducked out of the door.

As she let herself out, she heard Mrs Hollins come through from the shop and she suddenly remembered that she had not made Keith tidy up. Now it was too late to do anything, and the explosion was audible all through the house.

'Keith Hollins! You're like a baby, scattering papers everywhere. And it's no good trying to call it work. Reading newspapers is never work. Get them picked up at once!'

Keith mumbled something apologetic and Jinny squirmed.

She knew just how he would be looking. Stupid and shambling and guilty.

'And when you've done that,' Mrs Hollins shouted, 'You can just take yourself upstairs and make your bed again. Call that *made*? A six-year-old could do better. I've taken all the covers off and put them on the floor.'

For a moment, Jinny was tempted to go back and help Keith. He was so *soft*. He never stood up to his mother. It was nothing to her that he was clever and kind and gentle. All she could see was his untidiness. And because that was what she saw, it was what he saw himself. It wasn't *fair*.

But then she remembered that she was annoyed with him herself, because he had made nothing out of her mystery and her worries. So she closed the door and went back to her own house. And the beans.

11.00 a.m.

Tug lay on the bed with his hands behind his head, staring dully at the ceiling. Not quite awake and not quite asleep. Floating in the strange, exhausted doze that was all he could manage with the music coming, grotesque and slow, from the other side of the door.

Last night they had begun to play it at half speed. For a quarter of an hour he had been relieved. It was not so shrill on the high notes. Not so sharp on the clashes. Then he realized why they had changed it. He had just been reaching the point when he was used to the old rhythm. He could ignore it. He would probably have gone to sleep in spite of it last night. But now it was different. It filled his head all over again, and there was no sleep. All over again, his brain had started to fit words to the tune. Only this time it was as though they were being sung by a very slow, stupid giant.

> *WEEL* MAY THE *KEEL* ROW,
> THE *KEEL* ROW, THE *KEEL* ROW,
> *KEEL* MAY THE *WEEL* ROW
> THAT *MY DADDY'S IN*.

His eyes slid listlessly over the ceiling, following the long, jagged crack across one corner. Tracing the brownish patch of damp that stained the left hand edge round the skylight.

> AS *I* CAME THROUGH *SANDGATE*,
> THROUGH *HANDGATE*, THROUGH *STANDGATE*.
> O *WEEL* MAY THE *LONGBOW* . . . .

Up behind the wardrobe, at the very top of the wall, a corner of the paper was falling away, hanging curled back. The line carried his eye down towards the wardrobe

AS *I* CAME THROUGH *WARD*ROBE,
THE *MIRROR*, THE *MIRROR* . . . .

— with that Tug-Doyle face hiding behind the door, ready to jump out at him if he opened it. He twisted, turning his face away, and saw the Woman, sitting on the wooden kitchen chair in front of the door. With her gun across her knees. It was different from Doyle's gun—long, like a rifle, with a wooden butt and a dark magazine of cartridges curving wickedly from its belly. She did not pretend to clean it or play with it. She simply held it, loaded and ready, while she sat restlessly fidgeting and staring at Tug.

Don't stare back. Don't be caught by those eyes. Eyes that watched and kept guard. Eyes that stared at you, while the long fingers choked and throttled and —

'You make me *sick!*'

The words were sudden and fierce and Tug's whole body jerked as they crashed into his ears. 'Wh — what?'

'You make me sick!' the Woman shouted again. 'Lying there! Why don't you *do* something?'

Tug stared muzzily at her. What she had said did not seem to make sense. 'I want to go home.'

'Waah!' She pulled a howling-baby face at him. Then she jumped up and strode across to the bed, glaring down at him. 'You could at least *talk*. Or practise yoga. Or — '

'I want to go home.'

She shrugged. 'Of course we'll go home. At the end of our holiday.'

'I want to go home. To my mother.'

Too far. He'd gone too far. The Woman's hand moved dangerously towards the gun. Then her eyes connected with his.

'At this rate you'll be going home to a psychiatrist. You'll

59

end up with a howling depression if you don't start doing things.'

AS *I* CAME THROUGH THE *MANGLE*, THE *MANGLE*, THE *MANGLE*....

'I want — ' He began to say it again, stubbornly. But his voice jammed in his throat and he knew he would start to cry if he said another word. He was stuck, speechless and stupid, staring up into the Woman's eyes. She only had to push it, to try and make him say something else, and the whole world would slip away in a great wail and a wash of tears.

But she didn't. Instead, she caught at his shoulder and shook it, jarring yesterday's bruises.

'Stop it! D'you hear me? Stop it! Wake up and *do* something, you little toad. Come on!'

He did not know why she had lost her temper, but he could hear the rage in her voice and feel the painful grip of her fingers. Terrified, he lay there thinking, *Any moment now it will be the end. She'll raise her gun and —*

But just as her fingers began to tremble, she let go and jumped backwards.

'Here! I'll show you what I think of you! *This* is what it makes me feel to watch you lying there.'

Tug turned. He had no idea what she meant. He half expected to be met by a bullet, but the Woman had tucked her gun under one arm. She was feeling in the pockets of her jeans. As he looked, she wrenched out an ordinary packet of children's wax crayons and took out the black one. Then she turned and began to scrawl on the wall beside the chest of drawers.

There was no picture in the scrawl. No pattern even. Just long, violent, ugly lines, scoring across the pretty pattern of blue forget-me-nots. And all the time she was yelling.

'Look, this is what I'd like to do to your face! And this! And this!'

It was mad and weird and terrifying. But not only

60

terrifying. Tug found himself breathing faster and out of his terror a sort of excitement rose. Yes. *Yes.* That was how he felt too. Black, scrawling angry. Fierce and destructive. His fingers curled, longing to hold a crayon.

As he thought it, as if she had read his mind, the Woman threw the black crayon at him.

'Go on then. *You* do it. Or are you just going to lie there and put up with whatever happens?'

He hesitated. Even now, when everything had gone mad, the idea of scribbling on someone else's wallpaper was shocking. He saw the Woman sneer and knew that she understood what was holding him back.

'Frightened of spoiling the *luvverly* wallpaper, are you?'

'*No!*' Suddenly all he wanted to do was to make a worse scribble than she had, blacken everything, spoil it, smash it. He began to scrape the crayon across the paper fiercely, drawing jagged lines like teeth that stretched from the chest of drawers to the door. Random at first and then coming together to make a face. A huge, grinning Dracula face with fangs dripping gouts of black blood, right down to the floor.

'Hah!' the Woman shouted. 'And this is you!'

She had the red crayon now and she drew furiously, better than he did, even though she took less trouble. A silly, sentimental clown face appeared, with pop eyes and a shock of hair over its forehead.

'That's *not* me!' Tug dived at it, pushing the black crayon backwards and forwards over the face until it was almost obliterated by thick, angry lines. While he was doing it, he could see the Woman doing the same to his Dracula. Blotting it out.

Well, she wasn't going to get away with that. He spun round, looking for a clean bit of paper, and dived for the big, blank space on the wall opposite the bed. Right. He knew what he was going to do this time. Ignoring the Woman, who had moved to the patch above the bed, he began to draw in a frenzy, the music roaring in his ears as the lines grew from floor to ceiling.

He had always been good at skeletons, ever since Hank gave him that biology book one Christmas. All the rest of it bored him, but the skeletons were fantastic and he had practised and practised until he could draw every bone in its right place. But now a demon had taken over his careful diagrams and everything grew longer, sharper and more jagged. Finger-bones curved into claws, eye-sockets gaped black as caverns in the staring skulls.

So that everything was perfectly clear, he gave the taller skeleton a thick thatch of black hair and wrote 'DOYLE' underneath. The other one had a long tail of hair, nearly to its feet. After a second's pause, he wrote 'MA' underneath it.

'There!' he yelled. 'That's what I think of you both!'

The Woman had finished too, and she slid off the bed and turned to look. 'Well, well, well,' she said slowly. 'So *that's* how you see your loving parents, is it? How interesting.'

Tug did not want her to be interested. He wanted her to be furious. Furious and hurt. Pushing past her, he looked up at the wall above the bed to see what she had drawn.

It was much more cruel than anything he had managed. There, just above his pillow, sat a fat, cross-eyed baby in a nappy, one corkscrew curl sticking up from its head and its thumb wedged firmly in its mouth. Smiling wickedly, the Woman leaned forward and wrote YOU underneath it.

Before Tug could think of a reply that would sound as though he did not care, the music swelled and Doyle stood in the doorway.

He raised his eyebrows.

The Woman blinked for a moment. Then she grinned and waved a hand at the two skeletons and the horrible baby. 'We've been playing Happy Families,' she shouted.

Doyle stared. Then a slow, cold smile spread across his face as the Woman leaned closer and whispered to him, pointing at the skeletons. He stretched out and gripped Tug's arm, pulling him near. 'So you do understand about happy families after all.'

Tug was much too confused to reply, and Doyle did not

wait for an answer. He turned to the Woman and began to make arrangements.

'It's time to fetch the papers. Shall I lock you in and take the key?'

'No.' She shook her head firmly. 'Think I want to be trapped? I'll lock you out and you can hammer on the door when you come back.' She glanced over her shoulder at Tug as they went out. 'I'll only be a minute. Don't you dare move.'

Half an hour ago, he would simply have obeyed her. Would have lain on his back staring up at the crack in the ceiling and letting the sound of the stupid giant's voice take over his mind. But now his blood seemed to be flowing twice as fast. He was keyed up and longing for something to do. Turning the black crayon over and over in his hand, he wondered whether to draw another picture. But that frenzy had left him. And anyway there were no clear patches of wallpaper left. Not unless he pulled off the hanging piece behind the wardrobe and drew on that.

Not unless he pulled off . . . .

The idea came to him in a single burst, sudden and crystal clear. He did not have time to think it over or decide whether it was wise. He simply stood on tiptoe and pulled at the hanging corner of the paper. It tore away, leaving a bare patch down behind the wardrobe, where no one would notice it if he was lucky.

Hurry, hurry. His heart thudded so hard that the blood pounded in his ears and he was afraid that he would not hear the Woman coming back. He spread the piece of paper out and tore off the rough edges, to make a rectangle about twice as long as his hand. *Hurry, hurry.*

There was no time to think of the best message. He just scrawled the first words that came into his head and then began to fold the paper into a dart, sharpening the folds carefully. His hands shook so much that he had to concentrate as hard as he could.

When the dart was ready, he held it lightly, resting on the

palms of his hands, and thought, *I'm mad. I can't really be going to try and throw this.* It wasn't a game like chucking paper darts around in Maths. If he got caught, he risked a beating. Or something worse. For a second he was tempted to give up the idea. To crush the paper in his hands until it was a little crumpled ball and — and —

And what? He had trapped himself. The dart was even more dangerous to him if it stayed in the room. If They found it, They would know that he had been trying to escape. There was no way of getting rid of it except by eating it or by throwing it. And it had to be done *now*. Before it was too late.

Climbing lightly on to the bed, he wriggled his fingers through the bars and pushed the skylight open. Then he screwed his head round to peer at the lie of the land, the way the bank rose steep and wooded behind the house.

But he could not look and throw both at the same time. He had to move his head away, push his other arm through, being careful not to squash the dart, and throw from memory. No second chances. Shutting his eyes, he concentrated, not even letting himself listen for footsteps on the stairs, concentrated his whole energy and skill on a single flick of the wrist that sent the dart sailing away out of his hand.

Well, you've done it now, juggins. That's what Hank would have said. Pulling one of her funny faces. Tug pulled the face himself, just for her. Wherever she was. Then, shaking, he wriggled his arm out of the grid.

He was about to try and take a look, to see if he could see where the dart had landed, when he heard feet on the stairs. With the speed of automatic reaction, he slid off the bed. But he was trembling and breathless. Panic nearly choked him. She would guess! She was sure to guess. He felt as though what he had been doing was stamped on his forehead.

Then, just in time, he thought of it. He flung himself to the floor as he heard her key in the padlock and began to do press-ups. One . . . two . . . three . . . .

'That's better,' the Woman said, sitting down on the chair again. She settled her gun on her knees. 'Let's see how many you can do.'

She began to count in a steady voice and Tug went on pushing with his arms, rising and falling to the numbers.

'. . . seven . . . eight . . . .'

Gradually her voice settled down to a speed that fitted in with the stupid giant. Tug kept pace, pressing up and down, on and on, with his mind and body matched to the beat. He did not seem to be controlling the exercise himself. He was a clockwork toy, wound up by the music and the Woman's voice and set to push himself up and down, up and down, up and down . . . .

Day Five — Thursday 11th August

6.30 a.m.

'Where are you off to?' Joe shot out of the milking house as Jinny came past. Even in wellingtons, he could move as lightly as a squirrel.

Jinny looked down guiltily. 'Just thought I'd have a walk.'

Joe watched her for a second, his long finger delicately turning the gold ring in his ear. Then he shrugged. 'You can get in and do the milking. Then I should be able to get the roots hoed before breakfast. That'll put me half a morning ahead, and I could do with that.'

It wasn't *fair*. She had forced herself out of bed especially early, without waking Oz, just so that she could have a spare half-hour or so to take a walk up Back Clough Dale. And here was Joe, brushing her plans aside like cobwebs with the dew still on them, not even knowing what he was doing. He stood in the door of the milking house, holding out the buckets for her to take.

And she took them, of course. That was how she had been brought up. If there was work to do, you did it, with no lounging about. She went over to the big, old, white sink in the corner and Joe fetched out the hoe and vanished towards the vegetable field.

Jinny rubbed the cake of scratchy, home-made soap between the palms of her hands and scrubbed her fingernails carefully. Behind her, in the shadows, she could hear Florence making odd, bad-tempered cow-noises as she shifted about on the hard floor. When Jinny went over with a bowl of water to wash her udder, she stirred restlessly, flicking her tail.

'Oh, keep *still!*' Jinny slapped the big, golden rump.

'You've got nothing to moan about, you stupid cow. No work to do. Nothing but eat and sleep.'

She dried the udder and pulled the three-legged stool across, jamming the first bucket between her knees as she sat down, so that Florence could not kick it over. Then she buried her face in the warm flank and began to squeeze the teats rhythmically, talking to the cow in an undertone, as Joe did.

'Glorious to be a cow in the summer! Knee-deep in lovely cool grass. No call to move fast. No worries. And slaves to milk you when you get too full up. Mmm?'

'Moo-oo!' said Florence balefully, looking round. She was only half Jersey, and that half did not include her temper, which was chancy and morose. In that moo, Jinny caught an echo of the bellowing noise Florence had made earlier in the year when they took her calf away. She had kept everyone awake for a whole night and Oz had cried into his pillow.

And yet here Florence was now, munching away with her usual bad temper. The calf was sold long ago, and she would not even recognize it now if it ambled into the yard.

How restful, thought Jinny. If only people were the same, Harriet Shakespeare would not be staring up at a house where terrorists were holding her son. All that crying and fear would be saved and she would long ago have wandered off, swishing her tail, to find a better patch of grass.

As Jinny milked on, her thoughts floated vaguely, in the way that was one of the pleasures of the job. The thought of Harriet Shakespeare slipped into the thought of poor Keith standing awkward and miserable among his mess of papers, while his mother screamed at him for not being neat and ordinary, like Rachel.

From there, by natural progression, Jinny moved to the memory of herself, crying into Keith's comfortable jumper. Choking out the puzzle of that other mother and son. The boy in the attic who had cried, '*Help!*' and the lovely, lying Hare-woman.

That stopped the pleasant floating. She came up against the

unsolved riddle with a horrible jerk. If Joe had not caught her, she would be there now, walking up the dale to look down on the sleeping cottage. Wondering. Watching.

Only here she was instead, working as usual. Her bad temper came back. She was too well trained to take it out on Florence and she finished milking her, but she scowled as she lifted the heavy pails and carried them outside, lifting them into the water trough to cool. She turned Florence into the field and stood over the milk pails, stirring them slowly with a hazel stick. Round and round went the rich, creamy milk, as the cool spring water flowed past, down through the three sloping troughs and away out of the yard. Fragments of Jinny's face stared back from the broken surface of the water. A skinny, cross face with freckles and a thin, sandy plait.

Joe found her there when he came back from the vegetable field. He looked at her face, but he did not say anything, except, 'Get those pails into the dairy now. Otherwise you'll be late for breakfast and miss the Planning.'

Jinny sighed. If there was anything worse than being cross, she thought, it was being cross and having it ignored. But Joe was never one for thinking about what people felt. Only what they did. He would never ask her why she was pulling faces, in case it encouraged her to pull worse ones. Just for her own satisfaction she pulled the very worst one she could think of — worse than any of Oz's — with her cheeks blown out, her eyes crossed and the tip of her tongue protruding. Then she heaved the pails out of the trough and carried them into the dairy, pouring some of the milk carefully into wide pans for the cream to rise. Good, obedient Jinny. Doing as she was told.

All the same, she was late for breakfast. The others were there already in a circle round the kitchen table, munching their way through slices of wholemeal bread and thick collops of bacon. She slipped into the seat beside Oz and picked up her knife and fork.

'Good,' said Joe. He wiped his fingers on his piece of bread. 'Let's plan.'

It was their daily ritual. Every morning, rain or shine, school or holidays, they sat round at breakfast deciding what work had to be done that day and sharing it out. Normally, Jinny loved the Planning. She had a neat, methodical mind and it pleased her to hunt around for an odd half-hour or so to fill with planting lettuces or doing the mending.

But today was different. Today she had something of her own that she wanted to do and she felt trapped. Joe was quietly listing the day's tasks on his fingers.

'. . . someone'll have to go up to Top Piece, too, and have a go at that wall. It won't wait any longer.'

'Me!' said Oz. He liked walling. But Joe did not take any notice. They had not reached the time for sharing out. He just carried on.

'. . . and some time today I'll have to go into the village. See about getting some people to come up and help with the harvest next week. Tuesday'd be a good day, I think. If it's fine. That means you'd better sort out the hams and cheeses, Bella. Decide what you'll give them.'

Bella nodded. 'I'll make the extra bread on Monday, then.'

'How about cakes? You usually do cakes. They ought to be baked today.'

'Today?' Bella shrieked. 'But it's my butter day. And there's beans to be sliced. And if we want any bilberries bottled this year someone'll have to go out and pick them soon. And — '

'O.K.' Joe lifted his hand to stop her speaking. Bella always started each day in a frenzy of horror at how much had to be done. Then he stared down at the floor, gathering together the threads of the day.

When he looks up, thought Jinny, *he'll tell us all what to do and the day will be gone before it's properly started. Like yesterday.* All the day before, she had waited for half an hour to go off walking by herself and it had never come. Now it seemed that today would be the same. She wondered what it was like to wake in the morning and plan things for yourself. To choose.

'Right.' Joe looked up. 'Oz can do the chickens today. And when Jinny's finished the pigs she can do the butter. She's helped you often enough. It's time she did it by herself. And Oz can come walling with me.'

'*Good!*' said Oz, with his mouth full.

Jinny sat resentfully, mopping round and round her plate with the last piece of bread as Joe's voice went on and on.

'. . . and the bilberries can wait till tomorrow,' he finished. 'Then, if we're forward enough, Jinny and Oz can go off for the day with a couple of baskets. How's that?'

'Too much!' Jinny said, before she could stop herself. 'You've filled every minute I've got. Don't I get *any* time off?'

Joe was not smiling as he looked at her. 'You know it's busy getting things straight before harvest. Would you want to be lounging about while the rest of us are working?'

'No, but — '

'I'll tell you what.' He tugged gently at her plait. 'If you get through all right, I'll take you with me when I go down to the village after evening milking. You can drop in on Keith while I go round and see people. Yes?'

Jinny felt like shouting at him. Couldn't he *see* that he was just organizing her even more? But before she could say anything, Bella interrupted.

'When you two have finished, perhaps someone'll listen to me. I've got problems too.' She coughed and looked down at the floor. 'I've run out of sugar. I'll need to buy some if I'm making cakes and bottling bilberries.'

There was a horrible silence. Jinny picked up her mug and drank, to hide her face. It happened every time. Why wouldn't Bella learn? Joe hated people not to plan ahead. Especially when it meant spending money. His long, narrow face was tight and angry.

'How much?'

She shrugged. 'Depends on how many berries they pick. Three or four kilos ought to be enough, but I'll need some dried fruit as well if you want fruit cakes — '

'No. How much *money?*'

70

Even Oz was quiet, his eyes flickering from face to face. Bella avoided looking at Joe.

'Give me five pounds?'

He pushed his chair back from the table and walked over to the drawer in the dresser where they kept the cash-box. Counting out seven pound notes, he laid them carefully on the table. Then he counted the rest of the money in the box and frowned.

'Well, that's my work settled for tomorrow. I'll have to be in the workshop finishing that brooch. To see if I can get the money for it before the end of the month. Jinny'll have to do all the milking and start planting out the cabbages.'

Slam. *Thanks a lot*, Jinny thought. *That's right. Start getting rid of tomorrow as well.* Why did she have to be born into a mad, slave-driving family? Everyone else in her class would be spending the holidays riding or playing in the hills or lying in bed until midday. Even the people who lived on farms did not have to work like she did. Those farms were businesses, not monsters that devoured you.

Joe was already out of the kitchen and half-way across the yard and Bella began to put the dishes together. Now that she had the money she needed, she was singing happily.

> '. . . to plough and sow,
> To reap and mow,
> And be a farmer's bo-hoy-hoy,
> And be a farmer's boy.'

'That's what *I* feel like,' Jinny said bitterly as she lifted the pan of pigswill off the range.

'Way-hey!' Bella gave a squawk and grinned. 'Got the black sulks? What's the matter? Scared of making the butter by yourself?'

'No, of course not. It's *everything*.' Jinny put the bucket down ready to pour in the swill and began to tip the pan with steady hands. 'Honestly, Mum, don't you feel it too? We work and work and work — and what's it all *for*? We're horribly poor. All that fuss about the money! Other people spend that much on newspapers and magazines. I've seen them at the shop, paying their bills. They buy books and nice clothes and shop cakes and — '

Bella stopped in the middle of the kitchen with a huge pile of plates and said quietly, 'Is that what you *really* want? Lots of money to buy trash — and not work? Because we *could* have that, you know. All we've got to do is go back to London and get Joe to set up a workshop there and work himself silly. Like he was doing before. The rest of us could just sit and twiddle our thumbs and drink iced coffee. But perhaps you don't remember how he hated that life, and what a state it got him into. It was like a huge machine running away with him.'

Jinny was still not ready to stop sulking. 'So we all have to live like beggars so that Dad can have what he wants?'

'We're not beggars,' Bella said calmly. 'I could go upstairs this minute and drape myself in gold chains and beautiful bracelets.'

'But that's *different*.'

'No it's not.' Bella reached out a lazy hand and prodded at Oz. 'Go on, goggle-eyes. No need to neglect the chickens just because I'm talking to Jin.'

'That's right,' Oz moaned cheerfully. 'Force me out to work. There's laws against it, you know.' He ducked, as Bella aimed a swipe at him, and went out into the yard.

Putting the plates down, Bella sat in a chair and pulled Jinny towards her. 'Look Jin, what's up? It's not like you to moan. And you know why we're here as well as I do. Joe nearly had a nervous breakdown in London. I couldn't get him away from his bench. Even at midnight, he was still working. There was too much pressure. Too many other people were involved and he felt he was losing his grip. We came here so that we could be in control of our own lives and not tangled up with anyone else. We *chose* this life.'

'*You two* chose it, you mean,' said Jinny. 'No one asked me.'

Bella shook her head. 'You're like all children. You get the kind of life your parents choose until you're old enough to choose for yourself. And when you are, you'll be well-grown and independent. Twice as independent as most girls of your age.'

Jinny scowled and shuffled her feet. 'But what I want is a bit of time to myself. *Now.*'

'I know you do, love,' Bella said, patting her arm. 'And you've deserved it, too. But I don't think there'll be any to spare for a day or two. I'll tell you what, though. I'll try and wangle you out of the cabbages tomorrow—so you can go bilberrying all day. You'll have Oz, of course, but at least you'll be able to choose where you go. How's that?'

She smiled, but Jinny still felt wretched. She kicked at the chair-leg and the black, angry words burst out of her.

'It's always *Dad!* I don't want him to be unhappy and have a breakdown. Of course I don't. But whenever I try to lead a normal life, like anyone else of my age, he comes along with *another* job and *more* work. If he weren't there — '

She stopped, horrified at what she had been about to say. Waiting for Bella to be furious and upset. But there was no fury. Just a long, sad pause. Then Bella said gently. 'It's always the people you love who trap you like that, Jinny. If you didn't care about him, you'd just walk off and lead your own life. Do whatever you wanted to. It's because you love him that you feel like killing him and wiping him out of your life. But it's the wrong answer. If you kill the people you love — or run away from them — you only smash yourself in the end. You have to grow *round* them. Make space for how they are.'

Suddenly Jinny was calm. Because she saw that it was true. And, more than that, she saw that Bella was really talking about herself. This life was harder on her than on anyone else. She was totally unsuited to anything where she had to organize herself. Jinny swallowed her rage and tried to forget that she had wanted to go up to Back Clough Dale *today*. After all, they were all in it together. Family life.

This time, when Bella smiled and said, 'So — bilberrying tomorrow?' Jinny smiled back.

'Thanks, Mum. That'll be great.'

5.30 p.m.

Doyle looked at his watch and then up at Tug. When he spoke, his voice was raised just loud enough to carry over the low-pitched brass rumbles.

'Time to go downstairs.'

'What?'

Tug gaped at him. He had got used to being in this room, shut in by the four scrawled walls, the sloping ceiling and the unrelenting noise. With someone watching him all the time except when one of Them let the other out to fetch the papers. Was it really *possible* to go out?

Doyle did not repeat himself. Instead, he pulled the chair away and opened the door, gesturing with his gun for Tug to go through it. Sliding off the bed, Tug pushed his feet into his trainers and laced them up. Then, nervously and slowly, he walked to the doorway. As he passed Doyle, he looked up at him.

'Why?'

'Can't keep you cooped up all the time,' Doyle said, sounding amused. 'What sort of parents do you think we are?'

You're not my parents. Tug opened his mouth automatically, but for the first time since he had been there, he let the words go unsaid. Because he wanted to go downstairs. Looking up, he saw Doyle's small smile, and knew that the gap had been noticed. For a moment he was afraid. He had let something slide. Only a little thing, but he was frightened of where it might lead. Then his feet were on the stairs and he was walking down the narrow, dark steps, which twisted sharply to the right. Bracing himself, ready for whatever he might find at the bottom.

The stairs ended in a latched door. Tug pushed it open. At the same moment, at the top of the stairs, Doyle turned off the music.

It had not stopped, even for a second, over the two days. Now, in the sudden silence, Tug felt as though he had been stripped naked and pushed out into a football crowd. The tormenting music and the attic room were horrible — but this was more frightening.

'Go on,' Doyle said softly, coming down behind him.

Tug stared into a big kitchen/living-room full of old, heavy furniture that did not quite match. Facing him was the main front door, the door that led to the outside world. Beside it, a large window showed the first view that Tug had seen for five days. Close to the house, a narrow track ran up a slight slope. Beyond, in the distance, a great ridge rose high, running from one side of the window to the other. It looked massive and majestic in the evening light and Tug stood quite still for a second, imagining the wind blowing across its top. The free, cold wind.

Then Doyle pushed him and he stepped meekly into the room, noticing the heavy key in the front door and the two large bolts that were firmly shot at the top and bottom. They were not taking any chances.

It was obvious that his visit had been planned and was not merely a sudden idea of Doyle's. The Woman was sitting round to the right, beside a television, and as soon as she saw Tug she waved at a chair.

'Sit down. We thought we'd have a nice family evening in front of the television.'

They were both watching him. Big, hazel eyes and cold, blue ones. Watching him and waiting for something. Settling himself in one of the big, shabby armchairs, Tug gazed suspiciously at the television screen and waited for a picture to appear.

Even then, he had not got as far as thinking what would be

on at that time. It took him completely by surprise. He heard the music that introduced the News and all at once the screen was filled with a picture of his own house, a picture that nearly jolted him out of his skin.

Of course! He was News! People must be hunting all over the country for him. As the news-reader began to speak, he leaned forward eagerly, not caring about Doyle and the Woman.

'Good evening.' The television was not very good and the voice crackled and faded from time to time. 'The terrorists who are holding thirteen-year-old Liam Shakespeare hostage in his home in Shelley Grove have announced that they are members of Free People, the left-wing revolutionary group that aims to "break the tyranny of the blood tie and abolish the out-dated family unit."'

It was nonsense. Tug's eyes and ears blurred. Not one word of it made any sense at all to him. He must have gone mad or deaf. But the news-reader's voice went on, crackling but unmistakable, saying extraordinary things.

'The group has issued a communiqué setting out its general aims, but has not as yet made any specific demands. Liam's mother, Harriet Shakespeare, was interviewed at a friend's house today.'

Tug's eyes snapped back into focus and there was Hank, sitting in Mrs Mallory's front room. Her squashed-pekinese face looked peculiar, as though someone had smudged dusty shadows under the eyes and in the hollows of the cheeks. Her mouth was stiff in a familiar way, so that Tug knew she was trying not to cry. He wanted to be with her so much that he could hardly breathe. *Hank, Hank, come and get me out of here.*

'Have you been able to contact Liam directly at all?' said the invisible interviewer.

Hank shook her head. Her mouth was still tense, but her voice came out quite steady, as Tug had known it would. 'Not yet. There's a telephone link, of course, but we haven't managed to persuade the group to let Liam speak.'

'But you know that he is alive and unhurt?'

'We've glimpsed him moving around. Not very clearly, but he's certainly alive.'

Tug felt like a ghost, mouthing and gesturing on the outside of a window, in the darkness. Everything seemed to slip and slither round him — Doyle and the Woman, the dirty plates heaped round the sink, the vast, open view through the window. They swirled together as though they had been stirred with a spoon. But he gripped hard at the arms of his chair and forced himself to attend. He did not want to miss a word. Not while he could see Hank.

'Mrs Shakespeare, you are well-known for your investigations into extreme left-wing groups and terrorist organizations. Do you know much about Free People?'

The tough little face looked suddenly alert. 'I first noticed them when they carried out the hospital nursery raid about three years ago. Remember it? They swapped all the babies round and removed the name bands on their wrists. That's a typical Free People stunt. Not necessarily blood-thirsty, but making a point. They didn't injure anyone that time — not physically, at any rate — but there must be mothers in Yorkshire who are still wondering if the babies were really sorted out correctly.'

'But the group *can* be dangerous? There is real reason to be afraid for Liam's safety?'

'Of course there is!' snapped Harriet Shakespeare. 'You know that as well as I do, after the Beach Bombings.'

'Of course, of course.' The interviewer hesitated, and when he asked the next question he sounded faintly embarrassed. 'You have always insisted that groups like this should not be encouraged to take hostages. That no one should give in to their demands. Do you still feel the same now that your own son is involved?'

Harriet Shakespeare turned to face the camera directly.

'I hope I shall be strong enough to stick by my principles,' she said. Her voice was less controlled now. Tug could tell that she was desperately in earnest by the way she opened her eyes wide and by the little sudden lift of her eyebrows. It was a characteristic movement. 'But I also hope that people will understand what it's like standing outside your own house, knowing that your son is a prisoner in there and not being able to get in. It's very hard to bear.'

'And of course you don't yet know what the terrorists' demands will be, do you?'

The pause before Harriet Shakespeare spoke again was very, very short. Only someone who knew her very well would have noticed it. 'That's right. I haven't got any idea what they're going to ask for. We'll just have to wait and see.' She gave a tiny smile, brave but near tears, and then vanished from the screen.

It had been a moving interview. Touching. Intelligent. Courageous. And ending up with a thumping great lie.

Tug *knew* that that last bit about the terrorists' demands was a lie. He could tell, from the way she had hesitated and from the smile she had given. He went on staring at the television screen, not listening to the next item, but trying to work out the puzzle.

All through the first part of the interview — the crazy part, when she had been talking about seeing her son in the house — Hank had been telling the straight truth. No doubt about it. She believed every word she was saying. And when she was talking about the clash between her feelings and her principles, she had been desperately serious. But then suddenly — a lie. It was a hopeless jumble.

And the eyes were still there. Watching him. Waiting to see what he had made of it all.

Tug stared down at his shoes. 'Why did you bring me down to watch that?' he said gruffly.

The Woman leaned forward, her face eager, but it was Doyle who answered, dropping every word slowly so that it rippled like a stone in a pond.

'We thought you would be interested to hear about your friend.'

'My — friend?'

78

'Liam Shakespeare.'

'He's not a *friend* of mine — ' began Tug. Then he stopped. He saw Hank's face saying, *We've glimpsed him moving around.* All at once, he felt devastatingly weary. A thought slid into his mind. *I have been blotted out from the world.* He was too weak and confused and unhappy to fight it. Ridiculously, he longed for the attic room and the sound of 'The Keel Row', as if they were home. As if he had no place anywhere else. He stood up.

'I want to go back upstairs.'

The eyes stared. Then Doyle stood up too.

'I'll take you.' He put an arm round Tug's shoulders and the bare skin of his wrist lay warm and dry against Tug's upper arm, the crisp hairs tickling slightly. Tug found it repulsive, but he had not the energy to resist and he let Doyle lead him upstairs as a father leads a child.

8.00 p.m.

'I haven't got any idea what they're going to ask for. We'll just have to wait and see.' Harriet Shakespeare gave a wavering smile and Keith reached forward and switched off the video recorder. Then he looked at Jinny.

'There you are. You've seen my cuttings and you've seen what's been on the News the last couple of days. What do you think?'

Jinny was flummoxed. Only an hour ago she had been finishing the evening milking, peaceful in the milking house with Florence. But as soon as she walked in to see Keith he had faced her with a heap of newspaper and snippets of video-recordings. Dropped her knee-deep into the Harriet Shakespeare business and asked her to *think*. She looked round at the cuttings strewn on the floor and then back at the blank screen.

'Well — I don't know — it's sad. You have to feel sorry for

79

her. That bit about her son and her principles — you know exactly how she feels. And you've got to admire her for not collapsing.'

'In fact, she's the picture of a brave, devoted mother,' Keith said in an odd voice.

Jinny thought he was laughing at her. 'Yes!' she said fiercely. 'I know it sounds corny. You gripe about your mother and I gripe about mine. But mothers *are* wonderful, and it's something like this that makes you realize it.'

'That's *right*,' said Keith. He rubbed his chin and Jinny noticed that he needed a shave. 'These terrorists have really made a lovely picture by kidnapping Liam Shakespeare, haven't they? A picture of mother-love and devoted families. Let's all wipe our eyes.' He frowned. 'It's very, very peculiar. How can they have got it so wrong?'

'What do you mean *wrong*?' Jinny was too tired to try and work it out. 'Why should terrorists care what it looks like — as long as they get their money, or whatever they're after?'

'Terrorists hardly *ever* get what they're after.' Keith rubbed at his sweaty forehead, leaving a black smear from the newsprint on his hands. 'That's not what they're really doing.'

It sounded like one of his clever ideas. Jinny sighed. 'Come on then, genius. What *are* they really doing?'

'Well, they're not usually powerful enough to change things by themselves, see. Not directly. So they try to make pictures that will change people's minds. Like — let me see — like when the Palestinians once injected Israeli oranges with mercury in a supermarket. They told people there were thousands of poisoned oranges about. That they'd better stop buying Israeli. I don't suppose it damaged the Israeli economy much, but it put across just the picture the Palestinians were after. *Israel is poison.*'

'So?' said Jinny. She hated it when he made her feel stupid.

'So these terrorists are making a picture that says *Mothers are wonderful.*'

'What's wrong with that?'

'*Jinny!*' Keith pulled a face at her and tugged his hair despairingly. 'Why don't you oil your brains? Think what sort of group Free People are. *They* don't want to say *Mothers are wonderful*. They want to say *Smash the family*. Like they did in the Beach Bombings.'

'Beach Bombings?' Jinny felt weary. Was there no end to the things she hadn't heard of?

Keith sighed. 'It was last summer,' he said patiently. 'Crowded beaches, full of families sunning themselves. Then suddenly — POW! Bombs went off on six beaches at once. Blew about twenty families to bits and sent a shocking number of people scurrying away without their parents or their children. Free People claimed they had been "exploding the myth of the happy family". So you see the sort of people they are? Remember the communiqué they put out a couple of days ago? Look, here.'

Jinny remembered seeing it and slipping past it because it looked complicated and she was tired. Now she spread it on her knee and read it properly.

A Message from the Free People to their Comrades
Still in Prison

Comrades, it is time to wake and see your chains!

WOMEN open your eyes and see how you are chained to husbands and children. All the equal opportunities in the world cannot save you from the demands of your families.
THERE MUST BE A DIFFERENT PATTERN.

MEN open your eyes and see how you are chained to the capitalist system by the needs of your wives and children. As long as men have families, capitalists will be able to exploit them.
THERE MUST BE A DIFFERENT PATTERN.

81

*CHILDREN open your eyes and see how you are
chained to the needs and desires of your parents.
And while they force you to be what you do not
want to be, they are also teaching you how to be
parents. Shudder when you understand that you, in
your turn, will humiliate your aged parents and
bully and deform your children.*
THERE MUST BE A DIFFERENT PATTERN.

*The family is a primitive institution that gives the
rich an excuse to exploit the poor and prevents the
poor from resisting. There will be no justice and no
liberation until the vicious circle is broken and the
tyranny of the family is smashed.*

*The blood tie strangles the true brotherhood of
mankind.*
It is time for men to come out of the nursery.
The doors of the prison stand open.
The Free People will free people.

*In a few days we shall announce our exact
demands which must be fulfilled before we release
Liam Shakespeare. Be prepared to support these
demands!*

Help build the revolution NOW.

Jinny read it three times. Then, at random almost, she
picked up one of the other cuttings, which showed Harriet
Shakespeare's plain, squashed face looking white and distraught and pitiful as she leaned against a friend's arm.

'You're right,' she said slowly. 'It makes no sense. Why
have they done it?'

Keith leaned back in his chair and waggled his bare feet,
looking very pleased with himself. 'That's what I'm waiting
to find out. You know, it's turning out to be a brilliant story

82

to do. Thanks for thinking of it, Jin. I was amazed you'd even heard of it, to tell the truth.'

'*I* thought of it?' Jinny said. Then she remembered. Those big, golden eyes turned towards the radio, ignoring Mrs Hollins. 'Oh yes. The Hare-woman.'

'The *what?*' Keith sat up straight and stared at her.

She had not meant to say it out loud, but now that she had, she almost explained. Because she always had told Keith everything. Then it came back to her. *Find another fact or two*, he had said. And *Aha! It is the handsome stranger.* She tossed her plait over her shoulder and looked round at all the mess.

'Why don't we tidy up instead of yacketing on? Unless you *want* your mother to spend the rest of the evening raging at you.'

It was the first time she had ever warned him off anything private and for a moment he looked puzzled and embarrassed. But he was not a person who would ferret for secrets. With a meekness that made her feel mean, he knelt down on the floor and started to gather his cuttings together.

Day Six — Friday 12th August

2.00 a.m.

Tug woke suddenly in the dark, out of a nightmare of falling, of rushing water and ground that slipped away beneath his feet. He opened his eyes and was instantly aware of utter, spine-chilling silence. Everything was dark except for a single patch where the moon shone through the skylight on to the wall. A single pale, bright patch, from which two black skeletons leered down at him.

He caught his breath. At once, away to the side of the skeletons, a dark hump reared. A shadow moved across the brightness, coming towards his bed.

Tug screamed.

In mid-scream, he was choked into silence by a hand that came over his face, forcing his jaw shut. It was so dark that he could not see who was bending over him. *Let it be Doyle*, he thought frantically. *Not Her*. He could just imagine the Woman hitting him, smashing at his face in the dark with the butt of her gun. At least Doyle would not do that.

The dark figure bent nearer, too close for Tug to see the face. But he could feel its breath on his cheek.

Thank God, he thought, *it is Doyle*. And then he was doubly frightened, because he had known without seeing the face or hearing the voice, from small familiarities of feel and smell. As if he had known Doyle all his life.

'Quiet,' whispered the voice, very low. 'Daddy's going to tell you a bedtime story.'

Tug lay very still and concentrated on breathing and the voice went on, so softly that it was only just possible to hear it, even though Doyle's face was right up against his ear.

'Once upon a time, when Daddy was a little boy, he used to wake in the night and cry. Because he was afraid of the dark. Like you. Crying in the dark.'

I wasn't, Tug wanted to say. But there was something about Doyle's voice that made it impossible to interrupt. Something tense and hypnotic and terrifying. He lay there and listened as the voice whispered on.

'And when he cried, *his* Daddy would come. Always his Daddy. If his Mummy tried to come, she was sent away. And his Daddy used to bring things with him.'

Tug swallowed hard. The voice was calm and soft and the words were ordinary, but he knew he was being told a horror story.

'Sometimes it was a belt. Sometimes it was a lighted cigarette. Once—' the voice shook and hesitated for a moment ' — once it was a pair of pliers. But whatever it was, it had the same effect. Your Daddy learnt never, *never* to cry in the dark. Because his Daddy didn't like it.'

Tug's head was being forced backwards so that his throat was stretched almost unbearably. Just as he started to feel that he could not endure it any longer, that he would have to struggle, Doyle's fingers relaxed slightly. But his voice continued in the same frightful hiss.

'I've inherited that from my father. I don't like crying in the dark. What a pity *you* seem to have inherited *that* from me.'

Pain and choking and rage all came together at once and Tug twisted his head aside. 'I haven't inherited that from you!' he shouted. 'I haven't inherited anything from you. *You're not my father*. My father's dead!'

'You've inherited my fear of the dark,' Doyle hissed again, as though Tug had not spoken, 'But that's not the worst part. You'll have inherited the other thing, too. The hatred of crying in the dark. I'll beat you, just as my father beat me. And you'll beat your own children. And they'll beat theirs. On and on and on for ever, with no way out — '

'No! *No!*' Tug shrieked and struggled, trying to sit up.

85

'You're not my father! My father was Frank Shakespeare!'

But even while he was saying it, it did not sound true. How could *father* be any blurred shape on a photograph, too faded and far away to remember properly? *Father* was a huge figure bending over him in the dark. A deep voice. A rough chin brushing his cheek. And any minute, any second now, it would happen. Doyle would start to hit him and he would not be able to stop. Nor would Tug be able to stop shrieking. And it would go on and on and on —

Without any warning, the light flashed on.

'What the hell's happening?'

It was the Woman. She stood in the doorway with a man's night-shirt on and her hair in a plait. When no one answered her, she came stamping into the room with a scowl on her face.

'I said what's *happening*? I thought it was my turn for a kip. But as soon as I get into bed and shut my eyes, this racket starts up. Can't you keep the kid quiet?'

'Just telling him a little story.' Doyle smiled slowly. 'About family life.'

He looked across at the Woman, so that she could share his smile, but she did not smile. She was staring at Tug. Suddenly she came across the room, the night-shirt flapping round her long, brown legs, and seized his shoulder.

'What's been getting to you?'

'I — ' Tug looked up at Doyle. 'I woke up,' he said weakly. 'I saw the skeletons and — ' To his surprise, he had to stop, in case he burst into tears. And he could feel himself shaking. The Woman nodded.

'Yes, they're pretty gruesome. I thought you'd got a bit carried away when you were drawing them.' She gripped his shoulder harder and pulled him up, out of bed. 'Come downstairs. I'll make you a hot drink.'

As they reached the door, she looked back at Doyle.

'Get some Blu-Tack and put up those posters I bought. Cover the scribbles over.'

She did not speak again until she and Tug were down in the

big kitchen. Then, as she bent over the stove, heating milk, she said casually, 'So, what was Doyle telling you, then?'

'He — ' Tug breathed harder. 'About his father.'

'Ah.' The Woman nodded, still with her back to him. 'And he frightened you?'

Tug was still cold with the shock of it, but all he said was, 'I didn't know. That he was like that. I thought he was — safe.'

She turned, laughing softly, as she put the cup of hot milk into his hands. 'That's not how I'd describe Doyle. Not *safe*.'

'But he doesn't get angry and rage like — '

'Like me?' the Woman said. For a moment she was very quiet, staring over his head, and her throat moved as she swallowed hard. Then she sat down beside Tug, put her elbows on the table and rested her chin in the palms of her hands. 'Oh no, Doyle's not like me. He never, never, *never* loses control. But don't kid yourself. That's a *very* angry man. And dangerous.'

Tug lowered his head and sipped. The milk was hot on the roof of his mouth and he was sharply aware of the Woman sitting there, the sleeves of the night-shirt falling away from her strong, brown forearms. Her eyes travelled from his face down to the mug which he held in his two hands. The surface of the milk shivered treacherously, betraying his trembling. Slowly she stretched out and cupped her own hands firmly round his, steadying and warming them. Tug felt his hectic heartbeat slow down and his pulse grow calm, as if he were a little child being comforted after a nightmare. And, like a little child, he stopped being careful and tense for a moment and said what was in his head, quite simply.

'Ma, what's going on? The really frightening thing is not understanding.'

Her eyes flickered. Then she reached up a hand and stroked his hair gently. 'I know it's hard,' she murmured. 'But it will be all right, I'm sure it will. And you *will* understand. In the end.'

The next moment she jumped up, almost angrily, as

though she had been trapped into a softness that she did not mean.

'Come on. Drink up and get back to bed.'

It was not until he was climbing the stairs in front of her that Tug realized suddenly, cold and clear, why her eyes had flickered before she answered. He had called her *Ma*, without being asked to. The thought appalled him so much that he went into the attic and slid back into bed without saying anything more to either of them. Without even looking at the posters which now covered the walls, hiding the crayoned pictures. The Woman gave him one look and then switched off the light and Doyle settled himself in the chair and sat silently in the shadows.

I called her Ma. The thought ran through Tug's head, over and over again. And it was worse than that. Sitting there in the kitchen, he had actually *felt* as though she were his mother. He could imagine sitting on her lap when he was smaller. Racing up in tears and clutching at her when he was hurt. Waking in the night to find her bending over him. Rolling over, he buried his face in the pillow and tried to get back his old picture of her — hard and tough and violent, the same all the way through. But a tiny, treacherous crack of doubt had opened in his mind. Until then, he had been sure of his memories, certain that he could not have forgotten his parents and everything that had happened to him and re-invented the whole of his life before he woke in the attic.

Only — was it really reasonable to think that the rest of the world was in league against him? It wasn't just Doyle and the Woman, after all, who were telling him that he was wrong. The television news-readers and the police and Hank — even Hank — were saying that Liam Shakespeare was shut up in his own home.

What was it they said about people who were convinced that the rest of the world was plotting against them?

Then, uncannily, Doyle spoke in the darkness. The only words he said before morning. He planted them in the silence with eerie precision, as though he had read Tug's mind.

'D'you realize how many people believe they're called *Shakespeare*? — In lunatic asylums, all over the country.'

5.00 p.m.

'Aw, Jin, that's *enough*,' Oz said. He was tired and crotchety, heaving his basket along with two hands. 'Mum'll faint if we pick any more.'

'Don't be such a mardy-baby.' Jinny knew that she was being mean. They had been out picking bilberries all day, stooping over the little tough bushes among the heather and separating the branches to find the fat, black berries with their bluish-misty sheen. All along the Great Edge, from the Castle Rock northwards, they had worked in the sun, with bent backs and aching arms. And Oz had worked just as hard as she had, not stopping to gaze down into the dale, but picking and picking until his fingers were stained blue-purple.

But now that they had reached the road at the dale head, he wanted to turn down it and go home. He was right, really. They had plenty of berries and there would be jobs ready and waiting for them. Only — that was not what Jinny had planned. *At least you'll be able to choose where you go*, Mum had said, giving her the day as a treat. Well, she chose to go on, up along the hump of moorland that looked down on Back Clough Dale.

She shifted the basket on her arm and crossed the road. 'Come *on*,' she called over her shoulder. 'You know there's more up behind Mrs Hollins's cottage. No one'll pick them unless we do. It's *waste* to leave them.'

Waste was a magic word in the Slattery family. It made Bella shriek and wave her 'arms about and it set Joe drumming his fingers on the table with that quiet disapproval that was worse than anything Bella could do. Oz gave in straight away and started to follow Jinny up the slope.

Looking back and seeing him trudging so patiently and

wearily, Jinny nearly changed her mind. Instead she said, 'If you catch up, I can show you where Dad and I took the hare.'

'And tell us how you did it?' Oz said quickly.

'If you promise not to go splitting all round the village.'

Oz formed his face into a solemn mask that would have been funny if Jinny had not been trying to keep him happy. As it was, she forced down her sense of humour and began to explain what Joe had done, how he had blocked the holes and netted the gate and chased the hare out with Ferry. There was nothing Oz liked better than finding out how to do some new thing. He attended without wavering as she took him round to the head of the little dale, above the cottage, pointing out the hare's field below them as they went.

When they were level with the trees behind the cottage, she gave Oz a little push. 'I'll do up here. You go lower down, in the trees. Be quicker if we split up.'

Oz edged carefully down the slope, crouching every now and then as he reached a little bilberry bush. Jinny found some nearer the top, in the open, where she could stand and peer down at the cottage.

It lay in its hollow, drowsy in the afternoon sun, its grey gritstone walls casting a short, black shadow. There was no movement, not even a twitch of the curtains, and no sound breaking the sleepy summer silence. Discouraged, Jinny bent to her picking, telling herself that she was stupid to expect faces at the window or dramatic voices calling.

At that moment, a voice did call, so that she jerked with shock. But it was only Oz. He shouted from the slope below her, sounding shrill and puzzled.

'Hey! Jin!'

She spun round, but she could not quite see him. He was somewhere a little to the left, in a cluster of small, scrubby trees.

'Ssh!' she hissed, as loudly as she dared. 'Don't forget there's visitors in the cottage. Don't go annoying them.'

It seemed that he had heard her, because there was silence again and Jinny turned back towards the little patch of bushes she was picking over. But before she could settle to it, there was a sudden scrambling and slithering at the bottom of the slope. Then Oz's voice again, sounding quite different.

'*JIN!*'

She knew that panicky, rising note. Laying her basket down, she ran towards the shriek, her feet slipping on the loose ground as she came under the trees, until she finished with an uncontrollable slide that landed her almost on top of Oz.

And the Hare-woman.

She had Oz by the shoulder and Jinny, tumbling nearly into her arms, said the first thing that came into her head.

'Mrs Doyle!'

'What?' The woman looked up, puzzled. Then she looked closer studying Jinny's face. 'Oh yes, I remember. The self-sufficiency girl.' And she grinned.

Jinny began to speak idiotically fast. 'This is my little brother. I hope he's not been annoying you. He's not bad considering he's only eight and — '

'Thanks!' said Oz. He wriggled his shoulder free and stepped backwards, away from the Hare-woman and closer to Jinny.

'What have you been doing?' Reluctantly, Jinny looked away from the woman so that she could inspect him. There did not seem to be any wounds or any broken bones. 'That was a terrific yell.'

'I heard the first one,' said the Hare-woman, watching them both. 'Thought he might have hurt himself or something so I came out to have a look. And I guess I frightened him.'

Jinny looked at Oz again. He didn't *seem* frightened. He was gazing at the woman with the strange, unblinking stare which meant he was working something out. 'What did you yell for, Oz?'

He let his breath out and said solemnly, 'I found some mushrooms. Look.' He pointed at the top of his basket. On top of the bilberries lay a few rather scrubby chanterelles, slightly battered. Quite an ordinary haul. Nothing to get excited about.

'You want to be careful with those,' the Hare-woman said. 'Don't want to land up in hospital.'

'Oh, Oz is good at fungi,' muttered Jinny absently, wondering. Why make such a fuss about a few miserable chanterelles?

'They're grand.' Earnestly, Oz scooped them out of the basket and held them towards the woman. 'Here. You have them. Because I disturbed you.'

'Oh no. That's O.K.'

'Please. I *want* you to have them.' He was doing his winsome act, almost fluttering his eyelashes at her. The Hare-woman looked sharply at him and then shrugged, taking the chanterelles into her hand too roughly, so that Jinny smelt the faint apricot smell they gave off.

'O.K. Thanks. Now — are you going on looking for more?'

'Oh no,' Oz said, before Jinny could answer. 'My basket's full of bilberries. We're going home now. Come on, Jin.'

He hauled the basket up the slope, towards the place where Jinny had been, so that she could retrieve hers, but he did not stop there. He walked straight back round the top of the little dale until they came down the slope to the road, well out of sight of the cottage. Then he sat down with a thump, his legs sticking straight out in front of him. Jinny squatted beside him.

'And what was all *that* about?' she said sharply. 'All that fuss about a few miserable mushrooms. And then you forced them on *her*. She obviously didn't want them. They'll go straight in the bin.'

'Oh — them,' Oz sounded scornful. 'Did you really think I was shouting about *them*? Mingy little things. No, I only said that to shut her up. Because I thought she was peculiar.'

'What d'you mean *peculiar*?' said Jinny angrily. But the hair on the back of her neck prickled to hear him saying it so calmly. Because the Hare-woman was lovely, but she *was* peculiar.

'She jumped me,' Oz said. 'Bounced out as soon as she heard me call you and came scrabbling up the slope. That's why I yelled the second time. I wanted you.'

'And what about the first time? The one that started all this off? If it wasn't the mushrooms, what set you shrieking?'

She could see that she had got to it at last. Oz looked important and mysterious, settling himself as though to tell a long story.

'I saw a flash of white through the bushes. Thought it might be a puff-ball. Remember when Dad found that puff-ball up there and Mum did it with bacon — ?'

'Yes, yes,' Jinny said impatiently. 'Go on.'

'*Well*, it wasn't a puff-ball.' He rummaged in his pocket and pulled out something damp and crumpled. 'Look!'

'Oh *Oz!* It's only a rotten paper dart.'

'You open it and look inside.' Oz sounded impressive and serious. Silly little boy. He was too old for stories like that and —

Then she opened the dart and saw the smudgy letters inside:

HELP I AM A PRISONER HERE.

She stared down at it for a long time. *That's just what you wanted*, half her mind was saying excitedly. But the other half was remembering how the Hare-woman had stood on the slope, staring with those wild, watchful eyes and saying *The self-sufficiency girl*, with that direct, lop-sided grin.

Oz tugged at her sleeve. 'What d'you think it's for?'

'Mmm?'

'*Jin!* Are you going to do anything about it?'

All of a sudden she decided. She stood up.

'Come on. We're going down to the village. We're going to see Keith's Dad.'

5.40 p.m.

Tug was suffocating. His head was jammed up against the back of the sofa, his cheek on the carpet and Doyle's hand clamped over his mouth. His whole body felt bruised from the speed at which Doyle had dragged him round and thrown him on to the floor when they heard the shout outside. The television news-reader's voice still rang across the room, sounding forlorn now that no one was listening.

'. . . Free People today announced what they are demanding in exchange for the release of Liam Shakespeare. They want the Government to abolish Child Benefit and all tax allowances for parents and use the money to set up full-time Community Homes for everyone under the age of sixteen. They claim that this will "break the harmful power of the nuclear family" and they have given the Government until next Friday to agree.'

Weird, thought Tug. He knew that he had been brought down specially to hear that, but it seemed to have nothing to do with him. Could have been a million miles away. All he could think of was that he wanted to sneeze. His nose was full of dust and he could not help himself.

'A — a — TCHOO!'

He spluttered into Doyle's hand.

'Filthy beast,' said Doyle. He did not move his fingers a millimetre.

Then they heard the front door open. 'It's O.K.,' the Woman's voice called.

Her hands were full of queer yellow mushroom things. She threw them on to the table and looked down at Doyle and Tug.

'You two having a wrestling match?'

Doyle smiled smoothly as he got to his feet. 'Part of growing up. Trying your strength against your Dad. Philip's got quite a way to go yet before he can beat me.' His fingers were still round Tug's wrists as he looked the Woman sharply up and down. 'So?'

94

She shrugged. 'Nothing. Only a couple of kids larking about. I've seen the girl before. She's local.'

'A girl?' Doyle suddenly went very still. 'About fourteen? Skinny and ginger, with a plait?'

'Well — yes.' The Woman frowned and Tug could almost feel her muscles tense. 'You've seen her too?'

'Exactly.' Doyle jerked at Tug's arms to bring him round to the table. 'It was her, last time. I think the three of us should sit down and have a little talk.'

Tug slumped into a chair and looked first to one side and then to the other. On his left, the Woman sat biting her thumb-nail, with eyes flickering warily. On his right, Doyle's pale blue eyes were steady under the black hair, his face doubly familiar and hated because Tug saw something very like it every time he looked into the mirror.

'Right,' said Doyle. 'Let's talk about visitors.'

The two of them leaned closer, across the table, and Tug found himself leaning forward too, as though he were helping to make their plan. As though the three of them were a group, defending itself against the outside world.

6.30 p.m.

'I see,' said Mr Hollins slowly. 'And what is it you want then, Jinny?'

He refolded the paper dart neatly and sent it skimming across the tea-table. Mrs Hollins tutted fussily and Keith bent to pick it up.

'She wants you to go up there of course, Dad,' he said. 'To see what's afoot.' He spoke a little impatiently, and his mother rounded on him.

'I won't have you speak to your father like that. And as for him going up Back Clough Dale and mithering the folk up there, and all for nothing — well, I reckon you've lost your brains, my lad, to think of such a thing. *And* you can get your

95

elbows off the table. I don't know what Jinny must think.'

You don't care a straw what I think, Jinny said inside her head. But she pressed her lips together and kept it in. No point in riling Mrs Hollins any further. *That* wouldn't help Keith. She fixed her eyes on Mr Hollins's face and waited for his answer.

But she had forgotten that Rachel would have to put her two pennorth in first. It was done with a scornful glance at Keith and then a grin of agreement at Mrs Hollins.

'Dad'll make himself look a great idiot if he goes up there, won't he, Mum? Keith's gone out of his wits bringing Jinny in with a tale like that.'

Jinny clutched hard at Oz's hand, biting her tongue. But she had no way of signalling to Keith, and she saw him frown ominously.

'That's rude, Rachel,' he said, firmly but softly. 'You'll make Jinny feel bad, and she's done no harm.'

'*And* I'll thank you not to tell your sister what to do!' Mrs Hollins jumped to her feet. 'Come on. Upstairs. I will not have you two bickering.'

'But I wasn't — '

'*Upstairs!*'

Red-faced, Keith pushed his chair back, looking large and ridiculous. Jinny saw Oz gaping in amazement and she kicked his foot. No point in making Keith feel worse. She stared down at her plate, embarrassed and angry.

'I'm sorry,' she said as Keith went out of the room. 'I had no call to come bursting into your tea like this. Disturbing you all. Only — when I found the note — '

'When *I* found the note — ' Oz interrupted her.

'Oh yes. When Oz found the note, we reckoned it might be — it might mean — ' She doubled her fists and looked frantically up at Mr Hollins. 'I'm not fooling, I promise. And there was the shout the other day, as well.'

Mr Hollins grinned suddenly. 'Calm down, girl. *I* know you're not fooling. Know you better than that. You're pure Slattery, to the bone, with never a joke in your body.'

'Well then?' Jinny looked hopeful.

'*Please!*' Oz said. He was sitting next to Mr Hollins and he looked solemnly at him. 'You should have been there when that woman came leaping out at me. Horrid it was.'

Mr Hollins rubbed a large hand over his large face.

'You're never going to listen to them?' said Mrs Hollins.

'We-ell,' he rubbed harder. 'It could be — just could be — Jinny's right and there *is* something queer going on up there. I'd best take a look, just to be on the safe side.'

'But they're our tenants,' Mrs Hollins snapped. '*My* tenants. I'll not have them put out.'

Her husband stood up to fetch his helmet. 'Tenants or no tenants, I've got my job to do. Come on, Jinny. I'll use you for an excuse. Then you can see if you've made a fuss for nothing.'

'And me!' Oz said quickly.

Mr Hollins rumpled his hair. 'I'm not running a Sunday School outing. You can stop here with Rachel.'

Oz pulled a terrible face. 'But I was the one who — '

Bending down quickly, Jinny whispered in his ear. 'It's no good going on. He won't take you. But you don't have to stop with Rachel and Mrs Hollins. Take yourself up to Keith and tell him I'll be back to say what happened.'

To her relief, Oz nodded and, as soon as they all took their eyes off him, he slid away from the tea-table and out of the room. Jinny followed Mr Hollins to his car.

He grinned at her as he switched the engine on. 'Do we need the siren? Blue lights flashing?' He was much jollier when Mrs Hollins was not there. Jinny grinned back.

'Like a proper policeman, you mean?'

'Cheeky young chip!' But he was teasing her absent-mindedly. His real thoughts were on something else and he fell silent as they pulled away from the Post Office and up the dale. He did not speak again until they were bumping up the track towards the cottage. Then he said suddenly. 'There's no call to go stirring folk for nothing. I think we'd best not speak about paper darts and cries for help. Eh?'

'But how will you — ?'

'Leave it to me, lass. Just keep your wits about you.'

As they got out of the car and walked across the yard, their feet scrunching on the stones, Jinny had a queer feeling that they were being watched. There was nothing to support it, no face at a window, no movement of a curtain, but when Mr Hollins knocked on the front door it opened immediately.

'Yes?' said the Hare-woman. Then she caught sight of Jinny and their eyes met. 'Oh, hallo.'

'Hallo,' Jinny said. She felt that she had given the whole thing away, that the Hare-woman's eyes would be able to read all her thoughts from her face and that single word. But if it was so, the woman gave no sign. She simply looked back at Mr Hollins, polite and expectant.

'Good evening, Mrs Doyle.' Mr Hollins stood square on the doorstep. 'I'm sorry to trouble you. Perhaps we might come in a minute?'

'Of course.' There was no hesitation. Not even the second's surprised pause that anyone might have made. Jinny and Mr Hollins stepped through the door straight into the big kitchen.

The room was full of the cheerful clutter of a family on holiday — books, maps and a camera flung on to the table. There was a faint stale smell, as though everything might not be as fanatically clean as Mrs Hollins liked it, but there was nothing odd to see.

The other two people in the room were sitting side by side on the old sofa. There was the man Jinny had seen before, with the cold blue eyes that almost made her shudder as she met them again, and there was a boy.

A boy with black hair and ice-blue eyes.

'I think you've met my husband before,' said the Hare-woman. 'And this is my son, Philip.'

They're like as twin lambs, was Jinny's first thought. Then she saw that that was not quite right, because their features were very different. Especially the mouths. The man's lips were narrow and pale where the boy's were full — almost

98

swollen. But that extraordinary colouring, the pale, pale eyes and the black hair, clearly marked out the two of them as father and son. All her images of a tiny waif locked in the attic seemed suddenly foolish and fantastic. This boy was sitting in a room with his parents, like anyone else. And no sign of chains or a whip or iron bars. She stared at the floor, turning pink and feeling so confused that she almost missed what Mr Hollins was saying.

'. . . embarrassing to have to trouble you like this, but we've had a bit of bother with the sheep hereabouts. There's been a strange dog out chasing them. Young Jinny here reckons she saw it heading up here yesterday. That right, Jinny?'

'Oh yes' Jinny looked up, gathering her wits. 'A little terrier. Like a Jack Russell. With a tattered ear.' (Was that overdoing it? Why was the boy staring at her so?)

'No dog here,' said the man. The question seemed to amuse him in some way. 'But perhaps you'd like to look over the house. Just to be on the safe side?'

'Well — thank you.' Mr Hollins looked surprised, but he was not ruffled. 'I reckon I will.' He got heavily to his feet. 'Save a lot of bother in the long run.'

The woman opened the door at the bottom of the stairs. 'I'll come with you. Not that you need showing the way, of course.'

As they began to climb, Jinny looked back towards the sofa and met the boy's eyes again. He was still gazing straight at her, without smiling or speaking. And there was something odd about his face. Something unexpected, but almost familiar. Was it that he looked so much like his father? Jinny tried to track it down, but it eluded her.

His father prodded him. 'Go on, Phil. The girl'll think you're thick. Talk to her. Make conversation.'

He said it with an odd, teasing leer, as though he were asking for something very difficult, and when the boy spoke he sounded awkward, his voice high and polite.

'Do you live in the village?'

'Not to say *in* the village,' Jinny said. 'We're up the dale a bit. We've got a little farm — more of a smallholding, really.'

'Oh?' With a visible effort, he tried again. 'You live there with your parents?'

Jinny nodded. 'And my brother Oz and my baby sister Louise.' The conversation was heavy, like a choking weight, and she plunged on, trying to get some reaction from the boy, to make it easier. 'We're cranks, you know. Grow all our own food and make our own clothes. We'd have our own generator too, only there's not a big enough head of water to our spring. My Dad's always talking about trying a windmill, but he's never managed it yet, so it's home-made tallow candles in the winter, to save the electricity. And they *stink*.'

What was wrong with the boy? He did not even force a grin. He seemed to have not the slightest interest in what she was saying. And yet he stared and stared and stared. Jinny rattled on, less from politeness than just to try and cover the terrible, wooden silence.

'We need a bit of money, of course. There's always rates and suchlike. So my Dad has a workshop. He's a jeweller by trade and — '

And then it happened. Feet sounded on the stairs. Mr Hollins and the Hare-woman coming down again. For a split second the man on the sofa glanced away, towards the noise. In that second, while Jinny was babbling on about Joe, the boy looked her straight in the eyes and spoke soundlessly, his lips shaping a single word.

Help.

There was no mistaking it. And he was obviously serious. His eyes were desperate. They widened even more and his eyebrows went up and down, with an odd little flicker, as though with the effort of forcing his message silently across the air to Jinny.

' — at the moment he's making a beautiful chain for a Mayoress down south.' Miraculously, her voice went on in a steady stream, without a quiver, while her mind tried to take in what had happened. What did he mean? And then the

Hare-woman was coming through the door at the bottom of the stairs and the man with the cold eyes was watching again.

'. . . very sorry to have troubled you,' Mr Hollins was saying.

The man shook his head. 'No trouble. Come again. Come every day, if you like.' He still sounded amused.

'Perhaps Philip'd like to come over to us,' Jinny broke in quickly, finding courage from somewhere.' It's grand fun with the pigs and the chickens and the cow and that. Not to count my sister Louise. She's the noisiest of all. But he'd be welcome to come. My brother Oz is desperate to have someone to play with, on account of the rest of us being girls. He says — '

It was Mr Hollins who stopped her. To her astonishment, he suddenly prodded her in the ribs. 'We'd best be going, Jinny.'

The warning in his voice was clear. Jinny was so amazed that she stopped speaking in the middle of a sentence and let him say goodbye and make their apologies all over again. She did not understand what he had meant until they were getting into the car.

'Sorry to haul you off, girl,' Mr Hollins said in a low voice, 'But I reckoned it would be more comfortable for everyone if I got you out afore they had to start making excuses. You weren't to know, but the boy's simple. Has fits, as well. That's why they keep themselves to themselves up there.'

Jinny hesitated. 'You mean he's mad?'

'Oh no.' Mr Hollins sounded shocked. 'Not mad. Just a bit simple, like a little child.' He clipped his seat-belt and turned on the engine. 'Had posters of Peter Rabbit and suchlike up in his room. And a thick cloth across the skylight, to help him sleep. Seems to need a deal of mollycoddling. His mother explained it all.' He put the car into gear and they slid away from the cottage. 'So that's the way of it, you see,' he finished kindly. 'It's often like that. Go to investigate one thing and you turn up another that you didn't expect, like as not. That's one thing I've learnt in the police force.'

'But — ' Jinny frowned, not quite ready yet to tell him

what had happened to her. 'Didn't you think they were a *peculiar* family?'

Before she could explain what she meant, Mr Hollins was laughing at her. 'Live in a box, don't you, up at that farm of yours? Want to get down into the world, lass. See how it is. *All* families are peculiar.'

'But that boy — '

'Come on, now. I told you the way of that.'

Jinny looked down at her feet and spoke very quickly, so that he could not interrupt her. 'He said "Help". When you were upstairs. And he said it secretly, so that his father didn't see.'

Mr Hollins steered round a pot-hole. 'There's no more I can do, Jinny. I'm not a psychiatrist or a social worker. Don't ask for miracles. I've come on your wild-goose chase and that's all I can do for you.'

'But — '

'But they're queer? So? That's a family. I've told you. Prod any family and you'll find queer happenings. That's another thing I've learnt in the police.'

His voice was quite kind, but it forbade any more questions and Jinny fell silent, looking back over her shoulder as they reached the lip of the little hollow.

There were the three figures, standing in the doorway of the cottage, watching them go. Philip stood between his parents. His father's arm was round his shoulders and his mother was ruffling his black hair. Dimly Jinny supposed that Mr Hollins was right. A family. That was what they were. And who was to know what went on in anyone else's family? It was just as Joe had been telling her all her life. Not her business.

7.15 p.m.

Tug watched the back of the police car bump its way up the

track. Gone. They'd gone, the policeman and the girl, and he felt miserable and confused.

Part of him was coldly aware of the bulge in Doyle's pocket — the gun which had made sure he would not scream and beg for help. *Coward! I'm a coward. I could have been free if I weren't a coward.*

But it wasn't that simple. The policeman and the girl had come on an ordinary routine visit. To the Doyle family. They had talked politely and gone away without noticing anything. Because they *believed* in the Doyle family. And somehow that made it more real. Tug shuddered. *I am Tug*, he said fiercely to himself, struggling to drag his memories closer around him. But they were ragged and insubstantial, with the lurid colours of fancy dress. How could they cover the sensible, everyday clothes of Philip Doyle?

> (Oh *I* am a *Doyle* now,
> A *Doyle* now, a *Doyle* now . . . .)

He shuddered again, and Doyle's arm tightened round his shoulders. 'Well, well.' The soft murmur echoed Tug's unhappiest thoughts. 'And what do you suppose Mr Pig and skinny Miss Ginger made of our happy family?'

The Woman turned, pulling the whole of the little group round with her so that they faced the house, towards the mirror which hung over the sofa.

'Look,' she said. 'That's what they saw.'

Tug looked. Their faces were reflected back, two black heads and one brown, close together. Doyle smiled slowly.

'A lovely composition.' He walked to the table and picked up the big Polaroid camera in its leather case. 'Stay there, looking out of the door. This thing's got a time-switch.'

Taking a chair, he set the camera up in the yard outside, bending over for a moment to fiddle with it.

'What's he doing?' Tug said tensely.

'You know Doyle and his holiday snaps,' said the Woman, her eyes grave.

103

Then he was back, sliding his arm nonchalantly round Tug's shoulders and smiling into the evening light.

'Say cheese, you two.'

'I won't—' Tug started to protest. But before he could move there was a click and Doyle was starting back towards the camera. With a wrench, Tug wriggled free of the Woman's arm and ran. Not out of the cottage — that would have been pointless, because Doyle barred the way — but back into the kitchen. Flinging himself on the carpet, he buried his head wretchedly in the sofa cushions.

After a moment, Doyle said, 'Don't you want to see it?'

'No, I don't.' Tug pushed his head deeper into the soft, musty cushions.

Doyle chuckled. 'Scared?'

Defiantly Tug raised his head. 'Of course I'm not scared. It's just — '

But he did not know himself what it was and the impossibility of explaining made him turn his head at last and look across at the bright, rectangular picture Doyle was holding out.

There they were, the three of them, in the doorway of the cottage, rather shadowy but plain enough. The Woman loomed over the group, tall and brown and smiling down at the two mops of black hair — one over a quizzical smile and the other over a scowl.

It was a classic holiday picture. The two parents with their rebellious adolescent son. Anyone could have guessed the relationship without a caption. Tug shut his eyes, screwing them up hard.

'It's a lie,' he said frantically, trying to convince himself.

Doyle smiled. 'The camera can't lie.'

'It can. It *has*.'

'Why?' The Woman's voice was cool and intelligent, not teasing like Doyle's. 'Tell us why.'

'The whole thing,' choked Tug, opening his eyes. 'The whole stinking happy family. It's a *lie!*'

'Of course it's a lie.' She sounded pleased to say it and Tug

104

stared at her, with a wild hope that she was going to explain everything to him. 'Of course it's a lie,' she said again. 'The whole *idea* of a happy family. All families are parasitic and destructive. I've told you. The family is a prison.'

It was like being given an ice-cube when you needed hot soup. Tug could have screamed. 'I didn't mean that rubbish.'

Her smile faded. 'Oh *Tug!* Haven't you understood anything?'

A sour, thick fear eddied in his throat. A fear beside which the fear of the gun was nothing — a game. 'What did you say?' He spoke very slowly.

'I said you haven't understood a thing. I've been struggling away, trying to help you — '

'No, not *that*.' He brushed it away impatiently. 'What did you *call* me?'

She hesitated, searching back to remember what she had said, and then she laughed. 'What? Oh, I called you Tug.' Her eyes shifted, glancing at Doyle and then flickering back. 'Don't you remember? It's the name I had for you when you were a baby.'

'No,' said Tug, in a low, horrified voice. A dense blackness swirled round him. *Tug, I am Tug*. It had been his defence against them. His secret self. 'No!'

'*Yes*,' said Doyle.

'Look.' The Woman suddenly reached for her big, shabby handbag. Doyle watched her riffle through a wad of papers as though she had taken him by surprise, and when she held up something for Tug to see he craned sideways so that he could glimpse it too.

It was another photograph. Old. It must have been old, because she was in the centre of it, the lines of her face less formed, the shape of her bones softer. Her hair was cut aggressively short, accentuating the sharp point of her jaw and she was cradling a very small baby. Her smile, as she gazed into the camera, was wry and mocking, as though it amused her to find herself in the traditional pose of a mother.

'Really?' murmured Doyle. 'Well, well, well.'

'Six weeks old,' said the Woman, watching Tug.

'No,' Tug said again. But it was a blind, wild reply. As though he had lashed out with both fists to keep off an attack. He wouldn't *let* it be true.

Suddenly he reached across and snatched the photograph out of the Woman's hand, ripping it in half and dropping the pieces on the floor. As though, ridiculously, he could blot out the misery in his mind by destroying a picture.

Then he looked up and for a moment he was so amazed that he forgot the misery. He saw that he had really hurt the Woman. Hurt her beyond all pretending. She went rigid, her eyes wide and the blood sucked out of her face.

'How *interesting*,' crooned Doyle.

'It's not — it doesn't matter,' the Woman said harshly. 'It was only a photograph, for God's sake.'

But she was not looking at it. She was looking resolutely away, so that Tug could feel what an effort it took her not to bend down and pick up the pieces.

'How *touching*,' Doyle said coldly. He stooped and picked up the torn halves himself. 'Been cherishing this, have you?'

'It was only a *photograph*,' the Woman said again, as though she were defending herself.

They seemed to have forgotten Tug. Whatever the point of the conversation was, it held them both tense, their eyes staring until there seemed almost to be an invisible bond.

Then, very slowly and deliberately, Doyle tore the two halves of the photograph across and across, into a shower of tiny pieces that fell through his fingers on to the floor. The Woman said nothing, but her face was white and her eyes glittered terribly. Tug found that his fury had gone and he was feeling sorry for her. Nervously, he touched her hand.

'I'm sorry.' And then, because he thought she would like it, 'I'm sorry, Ma.'

But she turned away without looking at him and the next moment Doyle had him by the arm and was hauling him upstairs.

Tug went miserably, without resisting. The struggle in his

106

head was so fierce that he had no energy left to fight Doyle. Images appeared in his brain, one overlaying another, confusing him. The Woman smashing him to the ground and beating at his face. In the kitchen, with her hands cradling his. As he had just left her. How did you put all those pictures together to make a whole person? And — worse — how did you ever decide what you felt about that person or what she meant to you?

Doyle thrust him into the attic and locked the door, not bothering to stay and guard him. The room was darkened by the cloth they had pinned over the skylight, to hide the bars, and Peter Rabbit and Mrs Tiggywinkle and Jemima Puddleduck stared down from the posters on the walls. But Tug did not even look at them. He walked across to the bed and flung himself on it. *Oh Hank*, he thought, *what would you do now? Could you understand what's going on?*

But Hank would not come. He strained to conjure up her face and her voice, but they had vanished, as completely as though the memory had been cut out of his brain.

And the more he tried to visualise her, the more he saw another face. With brown hair, scragged back into an elastic band, and huge, golden eyes.

Day Eight — Sunday 14th August

10.00 a.m.

Jinny would have been quite all right. Back to normal and ready to forget about the Hare-woman and the Back Clough Dale cottage. Ready to concentrate on milking and hoeing and clearing away the broad beans and planting out the rest of the cabbages, so that everything was done before the harvest on Tuesday.

Only she could not stop seeing the strange boy's face.

All through Saturday, she worked on it, telling herself that it was none of her business. That the boy was just simple and given to playing stupid jokes.

But it did not work. Wherever she looked, the face stared back at her. The pale blue eyes gazed from the bottom of the milk pan she was scrubbing, piercing the clouds of steam from the boiling water with the quick, earnest flicker of their eyebrows. They danced in front of her as she went up Long Field, following Joe and the horse and heaving old broad bean haulms into the cart. They glimmered reproachfully out of Florence's golden face when Jinny sat down to do the evening milking. And it was not the memory of their silent, desperate appeal that worried her. That *could* have been a game, after all. Just possibly. What disturbed her was the feeling, at the back of her mind, that there was something she ought to have understood. Something that she would have grasped, if it weren't for her own stupidity.

She fought the feeling all through Saturday, but by Sunday she had had enough. She was sweeping out the yard while Bella cooked the lunch and sang to the baby. Joe was up in Long Field with Oz and the cabbage plants, expecting Jinny to join him. And she would have gone. But as she swept, gritting her teeth and ignoring thoughts of the Doyle family, a rich, delicious smell floated out over the yard. A rare, special smell that should have had her licking her lips and counting the hours until lunch.

Bella was cooking the hare.

For some reason that Jinny did not quite understand, it was the last straw. Marching across the yard, she put the broom in the tool-house and simply went on walking, towards the village and Keith.

As she went round to the back of the Post Office, she could hear Mrs Hollins and Rachel in the kitchen, giggling and chattering while they cooked *their* Sunday lunch. They sounded quite pleasant when they were alone together, without Keith to nag at, but Jinny still did not want to meet them. She could see Keith, crouched over his papers, and she rapped on the living-room window to tell him to let her in.

When he opened the door, he was grinning with surprise and delight. 'Jinny, you're psychic! I was just wondering if there would be time to fetch you down here before lunch. I need to ask you about something.'

'And I want —' began Jinny. But Keith was already pushing her into the living-room, bubbling with what he had to say.

'Sit there, where you can see the television. I want to play you a recording I made last night. See if you think it's as peculiar as I do.'

Oh no, Jinny thought as he bent down to fiddle with the controls of the video recorder. *Not more of this Harriet Shakespeare stuff.* 'Look I've not got long, and I want to —'

'Won't take a *minute*,' Keith said firmly. 'Listen — you know how worried she sounded when she was interviewed the other day? When she didn't know about the terrorists' demands?'

He didn't bother to say who he was talking about now, Jinny noticed. It was just She. He was obsessed.

Then she remembered, with grudging fairness, that it was

109

an obsession of her own that had brought her down there. Keith must be as bored with the Hare-woman and her family as she was with Harriet Shakespeare. She would have to listen to him first. Dragging up her last shreds of interest, she nodded.

'Well, the terrorists have announced their demands now.' Keith looked round at her. 'I don't suppose the news has got up your hillside though.'

'Don't be snide,' Jinny said primly.

Keith grinned. 'I thought not.' Then he looked serious. 'Well, I can tell you what they've asked for. They want Community Homes to be set up for everyone under sixteen. So children don't have to live with their families. And the whole system's supposed to be funded by abolishing Child Benefit and the tax allowances people get for their children.'

Jinny shrugged. 'So? That's just crazy.'

'No it's not.' Keith shook his head. 'It's exactly the kind of demand I expected. Very definite and precise and practical.'

'But they must know they'll never get it,' Jinny said. 'It's too *much*.'

'Of course they'll not get it,' said Keith. 'This time. But they're making dead sure people think seriously about the idea. By saying they'll shoot Liam Shakespeare if the Government don't agree by Friday. And that makes him as good as dead now. So — ' He stopped and took a deep breath.

Thank goodness, thought Jinny. *We're getting to the point.*

' — so how would you expect Harriet Shakespeare to feel now?'

'Well, worse, of course.' Jinny could not understand why he was asking something so obvious. 'She *must* have been hoping they'd ask for something she could give. Even though she doesn't approve of giving in. If they've asked for really impossible things, it means the whole siege has been done for publicity — and they'll probably kill Liam whatever happens. And she can't do anything to stop them, because she's not the Government.'

'*Exactly.*' Keith beamed at her, as though she had passed

110

an exam. 'Now, have a look at this interview that was on the News last night.' He pressed a switch.

The recording started with the news-reader announcing that Harriet Shakespeare had replied to Free People's demands. Then her fair, tough face appeared on the screen.

('She doesn't *look* any different,' muttered Jinny.

'Ssh! Listen!')

'Mrs Shakespeare,' said the interviewer, 'now that we know what the terrorists are asking in return for your son's life, has your view of the situation changed?'

'The demands are what I would have expected,' Harriet Shakespeare said steadily. 'I have spent the last six months investigating Free People, and what they have asked for constitutes the first stage of their long-term programme.'

'And are they a violent group? Do you expect them to kill Liam, as they threaten, if they don't get what they ask for?'

('That's an insensitive question if you like,' hissed Keith.

'Perhaps they think she can take it because she's an interviewer herself.'

'*Sssh!*')

'. . . not really wise for me to comment,' Harriet Shakespeare was saying. 'But there's one thing I do want to say. I'm told that the television is on most of the time in my house — the police can detect it — and I want to say something to Liam, if he's watching.' Her pale blue eyes turned away from the interviewer and towards the camera. Jinny's skin seemed to twitch all over her body, but she did not know why. Harriet Shakespeare went on speaking, very slowly and emphatically. 'Don't give in. It's going to be all right. If it's in my power, you'll be quite safe on Friday, wherever you are. *I'll do everything in my power to get you out.* Just keep on being brave, that's all.'

Keith switched off. 'What do you think?'

'She was serious, wasn't she?' Jinny blinked. 'Not just saying that to cheer him up. She really believes she can get him out.' There was no mistaking the earnestness of those

111

pale blue eyes and the curious, characteristic flicker of the eyebrows.

. . . the curious, characteristic flicker of the eyebrows . . . .

Jinny sat back in her chair and swallowed hard. *I am going mad*, she thought. She swallowed harder. 'Please will you run it again?'

'What?' said Keith. 'Why — ?'

'*Run it again!*'

He gave her a puzzled glance and then shrugged and pressed the right switches. This time Jinny watched carefully. And she caught it twice. Harriet Shakespeare's desperately serious expression, with the eyes widening and the eyebrows flickering up and down. The expression that had been haunting her for nearly two days. There seemed to be a block in her chest so that she could not breathe properly. As Keith switched off the video recorder, she said, 'You've got a picture of Liam Shakespeare, haven't you?' She was so short of breath that it was an effort to speak.

'Jin, are you all right?'

'*Please*. A picture. No, not one of those.' He had reached for the file of grey newspaper photographs. One or two of them, taken through the windows of Harriet Shakespeare's house, showed a blurred back view of a fair-haired boy. 'I want a proper one, that shows his face. Didn't you have something from before the kidnap?'

'Oh, you mean the magazine article that Mam found. The one you spluttered over like an old colonel.' Keith grinned as he selected another file. 'Jinny, why not tell me what you're after? You look really peculiar. As though you're going to be sick.'

'I'll tell you in a minute,' Jinny said shortly. 'And I *shall* be sick unless you hurry up.' *It's impossible*, her mind was saying. *You're mad, you're mad, you're mad.*

'There you are, then.'

Keith tossed the article across to her. Three shiny pages folded together. Jinny remembered it clearly because it had been quite different from all the solemn newspaper cuttings

Keith had shown her, and she had stopped to make fun of one or two of Harriet Shakespeare's more nauseating remarks. Like — *It takes a lot of nerve to become a writer when your name's Shakespeare* and *In the sort of job I do, courage and truth are essential.*

As she unfolded the pages this time, looking for the picture of Harriet Shakespeare with her son, Jinny's hands were trembling. She had not really examined the boy's face before, because she was too busy making fun of the article. But she knew he was there, because she remembered thinking how mean his mother was to talk about him. Now she was praying that her idea was wrong, that she would find herself looking at someone totally unfamiliar. Because she had not the faintest idea what she would do if she were right.

There was the picture. *Harriet Shakespeare with her son Liam.* And the boy's face was not unfamiliar. It was different, because the hair was fair and the mouth was smiling, but the same pale blue eyes looked out at her. The same features.

'Well?' Keith said gently.

Jinny shut her eyes. Opened them again. 'Have you got a black felt pen? A fine one?'

He handed it to her, with a piece of paper. Jinny let the paper fall to the ground and, very carefully, began to colour in the fair hair around Liam Shakespeare's face.

'What are you doing? You've ruined it!' Keith tried to snatch the pen away from her and she slapped his hand so that he did not jog her.

'Shut up!' she hissed. Then she went on colouring very slowly and carefully, wondering all the time what she was going to do next.

When she had finished, she put the top on the pen and laid it down. Then she stared at the picture for a full minute. She could feel Keith watching her. Waiting.

'Liam Shakespeare's not in that house in London,' she said at last, in a small, level voice. 'He's here. In your Mam's cottage in Back Clough Dale.'

113

10.45 a.m.

Tug had forgotten what day it was until he heard the bells. He had been lying on his back, looking at the ceiling with his eyes out of focus, taking his pulse over and over again to keep his mind empty. Because there was no music now to fill it. Doyle and the Woman had left him in silence, watching him but not talking. Letting the questions fill his mind. The questions he could not answer and could not ignore.

Looking back, he saw that, for almost a week, he had kept himself going with little schemes and plots. Shouting to attract attention. Making paper darts. Trying to signal to the girl and the policeman. Like a baby, playing with plastic beakers on the edge of a volcano, or shuddering at tales of the Big Bad Wolf while monstrous murderers sharpened their knives at the door. And all the time he had been asking 'When can I go home?' But all that seemed almost like a simple happy life, now that he knew the real questions. The questions that everything around him was asking.

Doyle, the Woman, the television news-readers, Hank, the girl and the policeman — even his own face in the mirror — all told him that he was Philip Doyle. That Liam Shakespeare was a hostage in a house in Shelley Grove. And did he really believe that they were *all* wrong? Or all trying to trick him?

Was the whole world mad?

Could he be the only one who had got it right?

The questions had chased each other round and round, finding terrible answers, until he knew he would start to scream if he did not shut them out. So now he lay on his back and thought of nothing and took his pulse from time to time. Because *that* was true. That was the only thing he knew for certain about himself. He wasn't dead.

Then the bells started. Church bells, tumbling over each other in the peculiar, timeless, mathematical jumble that means *Sunday*. They caught him unprepared, before he could blank out his mind, making him remember the last time he had heard that sort of ringing, last Sunday.

114

He had been running, running as hard as he could to break his record for the five miles. And he had nearly given up. But then the sound of the church bells had lifted him, flooded him with a glorious, fierce determination, and his aching legs had flown along, pumped by some extra force, some last strength that he had never tapped before.

He closed his eyes. The memory was staggeringly clear, as though he had just heard those other bells, as though he were just surging forward in his final spurt, kicking for home.

I remember . . . .

No! The cautious part of his mind froze. It was a trick, leading him back into the same old treadmill. Hank, Ma, Doyle, Shelley Grove . . . . Memories tumbled together.

Last Sunday I went running, expecting Hank home in the evening. She'd been investigating one of her peculiar groups and she said there was about to be a break-through. We were going to have a special meal . . . .

No! No!

Last Sunday I drove here in the car with Ma and Doyle. When I got here, I fell over outside and knocked myself out. That's why I have to rest . . . .

No!

He gripped the sides of the bed and struggled to clear his mind again, to push out every memory, even the sharp, physical memory of the running. Running was a delusion, just like everything else. He couldn't trust it. He couldn't afford to believe that he had ever run like that, with such aching legs and such a flood of strength. It might not have happened. It might not have happened. It might not have happened it might not . . . .

Of course it did.

The voice in his mind was small and cool, above the struggle. And suddenly he saw that it was right. It had to be right. He sat up sharply. So did Doyle, on his chair by the door. Tug grinned feebly at him, shrugged and rolled over, turning his back so that Doyle could not watch his expression. Then he started to think hard.

115

There was no way he could be remembering that experience of running — of the joy and the pain and the total, ultimate effort — unless it had actually happened to him. Perhaps not last Sunday, and perhaps not on the way to Liam Shakespeare's front door, but it had happened. It was a part of him, as sure and certain as his pulse-beat.

And if he could be sure of that, there must be other things that he knew about himself. Other memories that were too sharp and real to be invented. He could build up a knowledge of who he was, piece by piece.

Slowly, testing every thought and every memory, he began to think about himself. And what he could be certain of.

He was fairly fit. He could tell that from his pulse-beat, which was only fifty-four when he was lying like this, on the bed, and from the hardness of his biceps when he bent his arm.

He hated bananas. Even thinking about their blotched yellow and black skins and their squidgy, floury middles made him want to throw up.

And he hated desiccated coconut.

And winkles.

He knew how to change the washer on a tap, and make pastry, and mend a bicycle puncture. He was sure, not only because he could have written out a set of instructions there and then, if he had had any paper, but because he could imagine all the minute details of doing those things. The soft, perished feel of the old washer which rubbed black on your fingers as you took it out of the tap. The way the pastry mixture clung to your hands if you mixed it with too much water. The lovely, tell-tale trail of bubbles that showed where the puncture was.

He probably learnt French at school (je m'appelle Je-Ne-Sais-Quoi) and possibly Spanish (no sé donde me encuentro) but not Russian (   ).

He must have spent a lot of time out in the sun — running? training? — because his watch had left a clear, sharp-edged mark on his tanned arm.

Ideas bombed at him from all directions. His heart thudded and he realized that he had begun to breathe faster, with excitement. He took his pulse again to calm himself (it had gone up to sixty-five) and then began to concentrate hard on gathering up the bits of himself. Bits that didn't depend on who he was or what family he belonged to.

He was still doing it over an hour later, frantically trying to remember everything and wishing he had somewhere to write it all down, when there was a sound of feet running up the stairs. The Woman pushed at the door, behind Doyle's chair, and when he moved sideways she stepped in. Doyle looked at his watch.

'Not your turn yet. Another hour to go.'

'I know. Came to tell you I've cooked some lunch, and — ' she hesitated.

'Well?' Doyle did not sound pleased.

The Woman put her chin up defiantly. 'Well, I'm sick of heaving trays up and down the stairs. And I bet you are too. Why don't you just bring Tug down and we'll all eat together?'

Doyle gave her a long stare. 'All right,' he said at last. 'Get up, Philip.'

Tug slid off the bed, watching them. Doyle seemed wary and the Woman had started to fidget with her long tail of hair, holding it in one hand and drawing it through the fingers of the other. She led the way downstairs and Tug followed her, feeling Doyle close behind him.

'I see,' said Doyle softly as they came out at the bottom of the stairs.

The big table had been covered with a checked table-cloth and set out tidily with cutlery and mats and glasses. There were two large vegetable dishes with lids on in the centre of the table and, beyond them, on an oval plate, was a roasted chicken, brown and shiny with stuffing oozing from one end.

Tug sat down where the Woman pointed, but Doyle began to walk round the room, peering at the table from all angles.

'*Very* elegant. Do we say grace?'

117

'Shut up, Doyle,' the Woman snapped.

He wandered over to the draining-board and looked into a jug. 'Custard!' he said in disgust. 'How bourgeois can you get?'

'For God's sake!' The Woman thumped the table with her fist and shouted. 'It's only a bloody *meal*. Not a political statement.'

Doyle looked at her coldly. 'Nothing is *only* itself. Everything has political overtones. As you very well know.'

Picking up the jug of custard, he walked across to the table and tipped it, steadily and deliberately. A thick, yellow stream ran on to the chicken and trickled down its sides, until it lay in a pool of custard.

Tug gasped. He glanced up at Doyle to see if it was meant to be a joke, but Doyle was not smiling.

'What's the matter, Philip?' he said evenly. 'Surprised? You shouldn't be. This is the traditional family Sunday lunch, and we're having the traditional family Sunday lunch-time row.'

The Woman stood up and faced him across the table. 'You're just making an idiot of yourself. Lousing up good food.'

'I'm reminding you of what family life is really like,' Doyle said. His eyes did not waver from her face. 'Before you get too sentimental about it. Sunday dinners were hell in my family. My father grilled us about what we had been doing all week. Worked himself into a frenzy and gave himself indigestion. We were dead lucky to get to bed without a belting on a Sunday.'

'Great,' the Woman said sarcastically. 'I really enjoy your happy childhood memories, Doyle.'

They were leaning forward facing each other, one on either side of Tug, looming over him. The Woman was breathing faster, but Doyle was cold and still.

'They're happier than *some* childhood memories,' he murmured. 'Better than one story I know, about a baby who cried at *every* meal. Even Sunday lunch. A baby who landed up with five broken ribs and a cracked skull and—'

The Woman leaned forward further and punched him hard, in the mouth. Her face had gone white and very pinched. Doyle's eyes narrowed and as he put one hand to his face the other slid dangerously to his jacket pocket.

Before he had time to think, Tug began to talk, quickly and nervously. 'Ma, I'm *hungry*. And when we've eaten — whatever's left to eat — I'd like to have a pen and some paper. There are some things I'd like to write down — '

For a second he thought the two of them were going to turn on him and hit him. Then slowly the tension began to seep away. The Woman unclenched her fists, gave a short laugh and sat down again. Doyle looked at Tug almost sadly and spoke not to him, but over his head, to the Woman.

'You see? Make a pattern and people step into it. As long as the pattern lasts. Don't *you* remember interrupting like that to stop your parents quarrelling?'

'Oh, sit down Doyle.' The Woman was busy peeling the custard-covered skin off the chicken. 'I've got what you mean. I'm not thick. But we might as well eat the food anyway.'

'*Delicious* chicken and custard,' murmured Doyle, pulling his chair out. 'What have I got afterwards, to go with my gravy?'

'Baked bananas.'

'Oh *Ma!*' Tug said it without thinking. Annoyed. 'You know I hate bananas. I'll be *sick.*'

'Don't be silly,' the Woman said briskly. 'Of course I haven't forgotten. There's a yogurt for you.'

Her knife sliced down into the breast of the chicken.

1.00 p.m.

'But you *must* listen, Mr Hollins.' Desperately, Jinny dragged at his arm. 'That boy was exactly like Liam Shakespeare except for the colour of his hair — '

'And you're just the spit of Queen Victoria,' Mr Hollins

119

said heavily. 'Or would be if you had white hair and put on a bit of weight. Oh, there's no use flapping that picture under my nose.' He pushed away the photograph of Liam Shakespeare that Jinny was holding out. 'It's all scribbled over.'

'But think when they came here — just at the time Liam Shakespeare disappeared — and — '

'Liam Shakespeare's not disappeared.' Mr Hollins's voice was still kind, but he was not budging at all. 'He's where all the world knows, in his own house with a couple of armed terrorists. Now leave me be, Jinny. I've come home to my dinner and I've not a lot of time to spare.'

Shaking her hand off his arm, he looked at Keith as he went into the dining-room. 'See her out, lad. Then come in to your meal.'

Jinny stood very quiet for a moment, with a fist pressed to her mouth. When she was sure she could talk without her voice cracking, she said, 'What can I *do*, Keith?'

'I know what most folk'd do,' he said quietly. 'Go home and forget it all.'

'So *you* don't properly believe me either?'

He waved his hands at her, to warn her to keep her voice down. 'That's not what I said. I know *you're* sure, and you're good at using your eyes. You wouldn't dream a likeness.'

'And no one's really seen that boy in Harriet Shakespeare's house,' Jinny said eagerly. 'Only a back view in the shadows.'

Keith nodded. But he still looked doubtful. 'But where's the point? Why pretend you're holding someone hostage when you've really carried him off?'

Jinny thought quickly. There *must* be a reason. Because she was certain that that was what had happened. 'Well, there's lots of publicity to a siege, isn't there? Pictures on television every night and headlines in the papers. But do they *work*? Do the terrorists get what they want?'

Keith chewed his lip, trying to remember. 'I think — there's a lot of pressure. Quite often they persuade them to give up the hostages. And sometimes they storm the place.'

120

He looked very thoughtful, his brows heavy over his eyes. 'You mean they get the best of both worlds this way.' He nodded slowly. 'Could be. And Harriet Shakespeare was definitely strange in that interview, wasn't she? What was it she said? *You'll be quite safe on Friday, wherever you are.* Do you think she *knows?* That he's not really there?'

'But wouldn't that make her — ?' began Jinny. Then stopped. Why argue? She wanted Keith to agree with her. Instead, she said, 'So what do we do? Phone up the London police?'

'No use doing that.' Keith shook his head. 'They'd just be straight through to Dad, if they took any notice of you. And we know what Dad would say.'

'Well what?' Jinny looked fiercely at him. 'You're not expecting me to go home and wait till they shoot that boy on Friday?'

Before Keith had time to answer, Mrs Hollins stuck her head round the dining-room door.

'Keith! What're you doing mooching about out there when the dinner's on the table?'

'My fault,' said Jinny. 'I'd best be gone.'

'Yes Mam,' muttered Keith. 'I'll be in in a second.' But when Jinny stepped towards the back door, he pushed her into the sitting-room instead. 'Not yet!' he hissed. 'I've got an idea. How we could get a message through about the boy here. Without bringing in the police.'

Jinny frowned down at him as he fell to his knees and started to root about in his files of cuttings. 'You mean — write to Harriet Shakespeare? Something like that?'

'Of course not!' Keith sounded shocked. 'Be terrible to go troubling her if we were wrong. No, I thought — her friend.' He took out the biggest picture of all, the one that showed a distraught Harriet Shakespeare supported by another woman. 'Read that and see what you think.'

'But I can't stop here. You'll get in a row, and — '

'There'll be a row anyway. *Read* it.'

Jinny looked down at the cutting. *A Mother's Grief,*

screamed the big, crude headline. Beneath it, Harriet Shakespeare's face was huge and haggard and she was leaning hard against the woman beside her. In spite of the sensational, unfeeling way it had been used, the picture was moving. Jinny stared at it. How could she go home and forget what she knew, when it mattered so much to someone else? As much as life and death.

Then she read the caption. *A mother in agony*, it gloated. *Shut out of her home and frantic with worry about her son, Harriet Shakespeare collapses in the arms of friend and neighbour Lucy Mallory.*

'It's foul.' Jinny shuddered. 'Just so their beastly readers can feel sorry for her.'

'Better than not caring at all,' said Keith. 'Anyway, I didn't give it to you so you could go drippy on me. Think. *Friend and neighbour*. This Lucy Mallory must live near Shelley Grove.'

'Well?'

Keith rumpled his hair despairingly. 'Well, dumbo, if we had a London street map and telephone directory, we could probably work out where she lives. Can't be that many Mallorys in the roads round there. All we need is a trip to the library in Matlock tomorrow.'

'But that'd take all day!' wailed Jinny. 'I can't possibly — '

The door opened suddenly and Rachel's coy face peered round it.

'*Don't* want to intrude on you two, but Mam's nearly purple. You'll be doing all the washing-up on your own, Keith, I can tell you. *And* getting half of it chucked back because it's not clean enough. She's in *that* sort of mood. You'll have to tear yourselves apart, you two. *So* sorry.'

Jinny went bright red and started towards the door so fast that Keith did not catch her up until she was outside on the path.

'Look!' he hissed. '*I'll* go to Matlock. But I won't make the phone call. If you want that done, you'll have to come down and do it yourself. Tomorrow night. Half-past nine?'

122

Jinny calculated quickly. 'Say ten.' She would have a good chance of sneaking out unnoticed by then.

Keith nodded and darted back to the house and Jinny walked on down the path, trying to ignore Rachel, who was in the doorway. But Rachel hated not to have the last word.

'Honest, Jin,' she called, 'I can't think what you see in that great lummock. Did you know he cuts his toe-nails in the bath?'

'Better than having claws like some people!' Jinny flung over her shoulder and ran.

But she knew that no amount of speed would save her. As she walked up the track towards her own house, she braced herself, ready for a row of her own. And the rich, savoury smell of the hare drifted down to meet her, turning her stomach.

4.00 p.m.

'You'd better hurry up with those exercises.' The Woman looked at her watch. 'Doyle said there'd be a meal at four.'

Tug swung his arms like windmills. 'Great. What is it? Jelly and chips? Porridge pie?'

The Woman's mouth twitched. 'Spaghetti and treacle.'

'Tomato soup sandwiches.' Tug's arms stopped and began to whirl the other way. 'Beefburger ice cream.'

For a second it looked as though she would go on with the game, but then she stopped smiling and her eyes slid away from his. 'It wasn't a joke yesterday, you know. It was serious.'

Did she think he was an idiot? As though anyone could have thought it was a joke, with Doyle's face set foul as a thunderstorm and the disgusting stream of custard ruining the meat. Tug looked at her scornfully. 'I'm not a baby, you know.' Sitting down on the edge of the bed, he began to draw circles in the air with the toes of his left foot. 'He was furious with you for making a special lunch. But why couldn't he *say* that? Why be so — so extravagant?'

'Because — oh, because you know what he's *like*. He doesn't think it's any use just telling people things. Because they can only see what's straight ahead of them. The things they've *always* seen. If you want to get them to look at something new, you've got to *make* them see.'

'Make them see what?' Tug said, puzzled. It did not seem to have much to do with custard.

'Oh — everything. The whole world.' The Woman waved her arms wide. 'Look, think of Doyle. For years he hated his

124

father — and he believed, deep down, that he was wicked himself, because even his own father hated *him*. And then, one day, he understood, and the whole world opened out. He was free. He said it was the most joyful moment of his life.'

Tug tried to imagine Doyle having a joyful moment. Difficult. And yet he could almost see it reflected in the Woman's wide eyes and her glowing, excited face. Certainly that moment of Doyle's was real to her. '*What* had he understood?' Tug said.

'That it wasn't his fault. Nor his father's. That it's *unnatural* for people to be tied up together in families for years and years. All those jealousies and demands and pressures — the stress is too much. That's what happened to me. That's why I — '

She broke off abruptly, but that did not make her silent. Swept on the flood of her own excitement, she simply changed course, banging her fist against the side of her chair in her eagerness to make him understand.

'*Animals* don't stay in families for ever, do they? And people don't need to either. But the system is encouraged by big business and governments, because if you've got a family you've got something to lose. It stops people fighting against capitalism and represssion. That's what we've got to make people see!'

She had been gesturing with one hand, to emphasize what she said. Now she stood up and began to march restlessly round the room, swinging her long gun by its handle.

'We've got to rip off the blinkers! Let in the light!'

There was something glorious about her — almost Viking — as she stood in the centre of the room, tall and thin and fierce. There should have been shouting and huge double-edged swords slicing the air, and giant bonfires with wild, roaring flames. Tug felt the call to join her, to leap to his feet and let himself be carried up on the tide, into a high and heroic world.

But, instead, he drew back, repelled and almost frightened by the flooding, uncontrolled wildness of the emotion. And

125

another voice spoke to him, in his head. Familiar and wry, but just as fierce in its own way. *If a speaker excites you — distrust him. And if he excites himself — distrust him a hundred times more.* Hank's voice. His whole nature answered to the warning. Yes. That was what he felt. He was a cautious, unheroic person, and Hank spoke for him.

Of course she did.

That was what she was *for*.

The thoughts dropped small and icy, into the very centre of him, paralysing all his senses. He did not hear what the Woman said next. He did not even see her face. Suddenly, all he was aware of was one single, frozen thought:

Hank was someone he had made up.

Oh sure, *Harriet Shakespeare* was a real person. He had seen her on television. But the Hank in his mind, the one who calmed him down and cheered him up and got him going in a sensible way — she was just the sort of fantasy mother you'd make up if your own mother was too strong, too passionate, too overwhelming. Like Ma. If she tried to squash out your cautious, unheroic side. Harriet Shakespeare was a real person, but perhaps Hank was only a part of himself, given a famous face. Perhaps he was like the people who think they're Napoleon, or that they're in love with the Queen. Mad Philip Doyle.

'Tug, are you all right?'

The Woman's voice came swimming out of a great blankness, forcing itself on him. She was sitting on the bed beside him, clutching his shoulders and looking almost frightened.

'What's the matter?'

He felt weak and shaking, as though he had just had a huge shock. For a moment he could not speak. She shook at his shoulders.

'Look, don't break down. Not now. Everything'll be all right. After tomorrow.'

But he did not take in the words. Could not begin to

understand them. Tomorrow? Tuesday? What had that got to do with anything? Her face loomed huge and strong and worried and he struggled with the dryness in his throat, trying to ask a question without knowing what it was.

'Ma — '

While he was still searching for the right question to ask, the sound of a key in the padlock made them both jump. The next second, the door swung open and Doyle was standing in the doorway, with a tray in his hands, looking at them both.

'What a *pretty* picture,' he said. 'A nice bit of mothering going on.'

The Woman had let go of Tug's shoulders as soon as the door opened. Now she stood up and pushed both hands into the pockets of her jeans. 'Don't be stupid. We were just talking.'

'I think,' Doyle murmured, 'that you have forgotten what you were meant to be doing.'

'Rubbish!'

'Then why — ' his voice was level and unpleasant ' — have you left the Kalashnikov on the bed? Where Philip can reach it?'

He was right. The gun lay on the covers, where she had put it down while they were talking. Tug had not even noticed. Her arms jerked out immediately to scoop it up. 'There's no harm done.'

'You know very well that it was extremely dangerous,' Doyle said coldly.

'I was only being a little bit kind—'

'You weren't being kind. You were being sentimental.'

They seemed to be trying to outstare each other. If that was so, Doyle won, because the Woman suddenly crossed the room, pushed past him and ran down the stairs.

'Here,' said Doyle. 'Have some food.'

He held the tray out. On it was a perfectly ordinary meal of beefburgers, mashed potato and peas, with a cup of tea and an apple.

'Thanks,' Tug said.

'Thanks — what?'

'Oh.' He had simply forgotten. 'Thanks Doyle.' Sitting on the edge of the bed, Tug balanced the tray on his knees and began to cut up the first beefburger. But his hands were shaking so much that he could hardly stop himself knocking the food off the plate.

9.50 p.m.

Jinny slid out of bed, pulled on a jersey and a pair of jeans and stood listening in the dark.

From the next room came the sound of Oz, snoring. He always lay flat on his back, with his arms flung out, making a noise that drowned out Louise's snufflings. Quite enough noise to cover the sound of Jinny's feet creeping out of her own room and across the landing. Good old Oz.

There were no voices coming from Joe and Bella's room. Usually, at this time, they were lying in bed talking. *Asleep already*, thought Jinny. Better and better. Very slowly, she began to go down the stairs, step by step, wincing every time one creaked and glancing over her shoulder every ten seconds or so.

She was so busy thinking about the people upstairs that she did not see the figure standing in the shadows of the kitchen doorway. Not until it stepped forward and Bella's voice said, 'Jinny!'

'Mum! You're still up!' Jinny stopped, trapped, and thought quickly. Then she went on down the stairs. 'Look, Mum,' she whispered, 'I have to go out. I *have* to. Just for about half an hour. Please don't stop me.'

'More strange sneakings?' Bella peered at her through the dark. 'And you're not going to tell me why?'

'It would take too long, honestly.' If she stopped to explain, Keith would be gone before she got to the telephone-box. 'But if you did know, you wouldn't stop me. You'd say it was all right. I promise.'

'I see.' Bella hesitated. 'And what about Dad?'

'Ah.' Jinny could not bring herself to tell the lie. She hung her head. 'You're right. He would stop me. Because — oh, because I'm trying to help someone outside the family. He'd say I'm snooping and interfering.' *Blast it*, she thought. *Now I've had it*. She wished she could see Bella's face properly, but the shadows were thick and all she could make out was the outline of a head.

Suddenly the head gave a brisk nod. 'All right. If you're not just doing something stupid. You have to do what you think is right, even if Joe and I don't always agree with you.' Bella stepped aside. 'But be careful. And come back quickly. I shan't sleep until you're in.'

'And you'll not tell Dad?'

'I didn't say that.' There was a soft chuckle in the darkness. 'Let's hope he's asleep.'

'Thanks Mum.' Jinny leaned across and kissed her lightly on the cheek. Then she let herself out of the door and walked through the yard, muttering quietly to Ferry, so that he would know who it was.

As she ran along the track to the road, she had an eerie sense that she was acting out something she had done before, but she could not pin it down until she reached the road and turned right, towards the village.

Last time it was left.

Then she remembered. Last time she had slipped out in the dark like this was on the night the Doyles had come, the night that had ended with a mystery and a death. For a second she could almost feel the warm slump of the hare's body, and its weight when it swung from her hand, heavy and loose, as she carried it home by the ears. She shuddered.

Then she was running towards the village, ignoring the small scutterings on the bank beside the road, her old sandals almost soundless on the tarmac.

The village windows were bright behind their curtains,

cosy and alive beneath the cold, black shadow of the Edge. Jinny wondered for the hundredth time what it was like to be in a family which sat up and watched the television of an evening. Played games and records and telephoned people, without feeling guilty about the electricity.

Keith was standing by the lighted telephone-box. Jinny saw him move his head and look at his watch and she called softly, 'Sorry I'm late. I got caught.'

'Caught?' Keith sounded puzzled. 'You mean you couldn't just say you were going for a walk?'

She passed it off as a joke, furious that she had given herself away. 'Don't forget it's the middle of the night to a Slattery. Come on. Let's get on with it before I fall asleep. Did you get the number?'

'Sort of.' They squeezed into the little, bright cubicle and Keith put a piece of paper down on the shelf. 'Here you are. There were two Mallorys nearby, I'm afraid. You'll have to try them both. I've lots of change. I went into the bank while I was in Matlock.'

He dropped a bank bag full of silver on to the shelf and Jinny stared, momentarily distracted.

'But that's *pounds*.'

'Only a fiver. There's no use in running out of money at the crucial moment.'

Only a fiver. Jinny remembered Bella and the sugar. What would Keith say if he really knew what it was like to be a Slattery?

'Come on, girl. Get going if you're going to do it.'

She lifted the receiver and dialled the first number with great care. Out in the darkness, she saw the Post Office door open and Mrs Hollins poke her head out. *Nosy.* Jinny smiled politely at her, listening to the ringing tone.

'Yes?' It was a man's voice, brisk and well-bred. Jinny was paralysed until Keith prodded her and she choked out the first words.

'Mr Mallory?'

'Speaking.'

'Could I — I mean — please can I give you a message for Harriet Shakespeare?'

'No you can't.' Suddenly the man on the phone was furious. 'For the last time, Harriet Shakespeare *is not here!* Good *night.*'

He banged the phone down and Jinny turned to Keith, shaking. 'He was—awful. Why did he have to be so rude?'

Keith grinned. He was near enough to hear everything. 'Looks like we're not the only people to work out this Mallory thing.' He took the receiver firmly out of her hand, listened for the dialling tone and dialled the second number. 'You going to do it then?'

'Yes.' She took the receiver and Keith put his face close again, so that he would not miss anything. The ringing seemed to go on and on and when at last a voice answered it took Jinny by surprise.

'What number are you calling?'

'What?' She looked stupidly at the telephone.

'This is the exchange,' said the voice. 'What number are you calling?'

Keith put his finger on the paper, beside the right one, and Jinny read it out.

'And who do you want to speak to?'

'Lucy Mallory.'

'What is your name?'

'Imogen Slattery.'

'And what number are you calling from?'

'Er — ' Jinny looked down at the dial. ' — Ashdale 623X'

'Hold the line, please.'

The ringing began again and Jinny covered the mouthpiece. 'What is it? What's going on?'

'Must have had their calls re-routed through the exchange,' Keith whispered back. 'To put off cranks and keep a record of who telephones. Looks like we've got the right number.' He pushed a couple more coins into the slot.

Then there was another voice. A woman's. 'Lucy Mallory.'

131

Jinny took a deep breath and felt her heart thud. 'Please — I want to give you a message for Harriet Shakespeare.'

At once the woman's voice went cold. 'Who is that speaking?'

'*Please*,' said Jinny desperately. 'I'm not a crank. It's important. It's about Liam. I want to tell you — '

'Wait a moment.' The woman did not sound any friendlier and the pause was a long one. Once they heard her say, 'But Harry, you can't keep on — ' And then she must have put a hand over the mouthpiece, because they did not hear anything else until, suddenly, another voice spoke.

'Hallo.'

A different voice. Deeper, and very clear. A voice that they had heard over and over again as they sat in Keith's sitting-room. Jinny gulped.

'You — you're Harriet Shakespeare!'

'That's right.'

'Look — ' There did not seem to be any way of wrapping it up. The words came bursting out anyhow. 'I know where Liam is.'

On the other end of the line, the voice hesitated and then went steely-hard. 'Everyone knows where Liam is.'

'But he's not.' Jinny gabbled it, trying to get it in before she was cut off. 'He's not in your house. He's in my village. Being kept a prisoner. I've seen him, only he's got black hair and—'

'Listen!' Harriet Shakespeare broke in, so fiercely that Jinny could imagine the fury on her face. 'You're the *fourteenth* person who's worked out I'm staying with Lucy and phoned me up with crazy stories about Liam. I suppose you must get a thrill out of it, but if you really knew anything you'd go to the police.'

'That's not fair!' Jinny shouted it. 'I've tried telling the police, but *they* still think Liam's in your house. It's no use talking to them.'

There was a silence. Then Harriet Shakespeare said, more

132

softly and sounding puzzled, 'So why is it any use talking to me?'

'Well — we saw your last interview. You seemed — that is we thought — that you knew something — '

'Yes?' The word was clipped short. Jinny hunted for what she wanted to say and then let it out in a rush.

'We thought you wouldn't have been like you were in that interview unless you knew something that — that you weren't telling people. We thought you might have guessed that all those announcements by the terrorists were a lie and really — '

'And?' Harriet Shakespeare said. All at once her voice was very low. Not angry, but quiet and tense. '*What* do I know that I'm not telling people?'

'That they're only pretending to have Liam in your house. 'That really he's somewhere else.'

'Oh.' It was long drawn out. Almost, Jinny could have sworn, on a breath of relief. And then she was angry again.

'You're wrong. You're quite wrong. Now why don't you just forget the whole thing? And stop imagining things about me!'

A click. And then the dialling tone. Very carefully, Jinny put the receiver back into its cradle.

'Well,' she said, and her voice came out high and cracking, 'we were wrong. She didn't know anything. She didn't understand at all. She was *horrible.*'

Keith patted her absent-mindedly on the shoulder. But he was not looking at her. He was staring out at the great dark sweep of the Edge, above the dale. 'I don't think we were wrong,' he said slowly. 'We were wrong about *what* she knew, I'll give you that. But she didn't like the idea that we knew she was hiding something, did she? I wonder what — ?'

And he went on gazing out of the window, drawing on it with his finger until Mrs Hollins came out and rapped on the glass.

2.55 a.m.

'Tug!'

The whisper made him stir in his sleep, turning and thrusting one arm under the pillow.

'*Tug!*'

This time the hiss was louder and strong fingers gripped his shoulder and shook it, jerking him awake. He opened his eyes in darkness and for a horrific moment he was completely adrift, not knowing what was happening or where — or who — he was. Nothing but blackness.

Then, under his pillow, his hand touched paper. The small, folded sheets on which he was writing down the things he knew about himself. The feel of them brought him back into the attic room, to the confusion that made a few words on a piece of paper into a lifeline.

He lifted his head.

'Tug?'

'Ma? What's up? What time is it?'

She leaned closer, her mouth almost on his ear. 'Ssh. Don't wake Doyle. I thought you'd want to hear this.'

Dimly he saw that she was holding something, but he did not realize what it was until she spoke again.

'Come on. Wake up properly. The next News is in a minute or two.'

Of course. It was the little radio that they listened to while they were on guard. But the Woman did not offer him the ear-piece that she and Doyle used. Instead, she turned it on so low that at first Tug could not make out anything except a faint crackling and hissing. He sat up and lifted the radio so

134

that it was close to his ear. Even so, the first words took him by surprise.

'Good morning.'

It was soft, but as brisk and clear as it would have been in the middle of the day. And then it went on and Tug stopped thinking about the quality of the sound. Because of what the news-reader was saying.

'There has been an extraordinary development in the Shelley Grove siege. Just before midnight last night, a special unit of police stormed the house, taking control of it and capturing the terrorists inside, without loss of life. However, they found no trace of Liam Shakespeare, whom the terrorists had claimed to be holding hostage.'

Tug's throat made a strange, clicking noise and the Woman's shadowy hand clutched at his. The voice of the news-reader flowed smoothly on.

'The terrorist group included a youth of about fifteen with bleached hair and it is thought that glimpses of this boy were used skilfully to support the terrorists' claims. No further information is available at present, but it is understood that police are interviewing the five people arrested.'

'Poor devils!' said the Woman. She clicked the radio off and sat quite still on the bed while Tug wondered what to say.

'What does it mean?' he said stupidly.

She snorted softly and he could imagine her smiling in the darkness. 'It means that they're beginning to realize that Free People are not just a bunch of dumb bomb-chuckers.'

'But what about me?'

She squeezed his hand again. 'You're all right. You're safe on holiday with your family. Harriet Shakespeare can't — '

She stopped. Tug shook at her hand. 'What? What were you going to say?'

But she would not go on. Pushing him back down into bed, she stood up, looming over him like the shadows of a nightmare.

'Listen, forget about Harriet Shakespeare. She's a hundred

135

and sixty miles away, in a different box. All *we* have to do is wait until this day is over.'

Today. Tuesday. 'Aren't you going to tell me — ?'

'No. Shut up now, or you'll wake Doyle.'

'But you can't just — '

'*Shut up.*'

There was something in her voice that reminded Tug that she was the one who had beaten him round the face. He rolled over, thinking resentfully that it was impossible to go to sleep. His head was jammed with questions — about Free People, about the siege, about Harriet Shakespeare. About today. How could he just —

The questions linked, separated, twisted themselves into fantastic jumbles and finally slid over into his sleeping mind, so that he dreamed, terrifyingly, that he was opening a never-ending stream of boxes. Some of them were beautiful, delicately lacquered or intricately carved, and some were rough old cardboard, stamped with code numbers. But inside each one was another and another and another . . . . The dream grew faster and faster and more and more desperate, because he knew that he had to reach the last box before the end of the day. But he was hindered by two things. One was Hank, who stood at his side, pulling his sleeve to make him stop. The other was the knowledge, inexplicable and certain, like all knowledge in dreams, that he would find something deadly inside the last box.

When he woke, sweating and exhausted, with his heart thudding as though he had been running, it was properly morning. The cloth over the skylight had been pulled aside, so that the room was bright. Blinking in the sunshine that fell on his face, Tug swam up out of the horrors of the darkness.

All the happenings of the night had mixed together so that he no longer knew whether he had really been woken and heard the Woman's hushed, hissing voice and the faint News from the radio. They seemed part of his dream, as unreal as the terrifying boxes. Was it really true that the house in Shelley Grove had been stormed? That Liam Shakespeare was missing? Perhaps he might be Liam Shakespeare after all. But —

But he could be Lord Lucan.

Or the crew of the *Marie Celeste*.

Or anyone else who had disappeared mysteriously. What he really felt was that Liam Shakespeare had been vaporized. Obliterated. That he—Tug—was left bare and unprotected, with nothing to prove who he was. Except the little bundle of papers folded together under his pillow.

6.45 a.m.

Jinny's head ached and her eyes were heavy and sore as though someone had punched them. *I didn't sleep a wink.* She had heard people say it often enough — she had even said it herself — but she had not realized what it would really be like.

To lie hour after hour in the same hot, crumpled bed, looking at the same crack of sky between the curtains. Watching the stars dim as it turned first grey and then pink. Hearing all the time, over and over again, the words of that disastrous, shaming telephone conversation.

I suppose you must get a thrill out of it . . . stop imagining things about me. She buried her head in Florence's flank and groaned. The old cow turned and licked her with a huge, wet tongue until her blouse was damp all over the right shoulder, but it was not comforting. It did not stop her knowing that she had made an idiot of herself and upset Harriet Shakespeare, who had enough trouble without that. Or that there was no way left of convincing anyone that she was right about that boy.

It did not occur to her for a moment that she might *not* be right. Ever since the first time she had seen the Hare-woman standing in the Post Office, staring with her luminous eyes as she told one lie after another, she had known that there was something wrong about her. Beautiful, but wrong. And ever since she had realized who the Doyle boy reminded her of, she had thought she knew what kind of thing was wrong. But she had bungled every single attempt to help.

Groaning again, she closed her eyes as her fingers squeezed and relaxed, and wondered why Florence was so hard to milk this morning. And Florence lowed reproachfully and flicked her tail, restless because her milker was tense.

Stopping at last to move the full bucket and reach for another, Jinny heard a car come bumping up the track towards the farm. Normally she would have wandered out to see who it was. Cars were rare on their track, especially at seven o'clock in the morning. And anyone who came calling at that time today must have more time than sense, because today was Tuesday. And all the village knew that the Slatterys were harvesting this Tuesday. The place would be in a rush and a turmoil until they were all out in the field and Joe was sure enough of the neighbours who had come to help.

But Jinny simply did not have the energy to investigate the car. If she stopped milking, she would never start again. So she kept her eyes closed, humming a little tune to try and make Florence let her milk down faster and barely listening to the sound of voices out in the yard.

'Still milking?' That was Joe. He appeared suddenly in the door of the milking house looking long and sallow and disapproving.

'It's not my fault. I started on time but I can't — '

'Oh, never mind.' His fingers flicked, brushing her excuses away. 'You've got a visitor.'

So that was why he was so bad-tempered. Jinny supposed it was Keith and she looked round, ready to make sure he knew how stupid he was to come now.

Only it was not Keith. It was a woman in sun-glasses, the collar of her short, smart coat turned up against the morning mist. She nodded dismissively at Joe, who glared and stamped back to the pigs, and then she came into the milking house and leaned against the far wall, looking across at Jinny.

And still Jinny did not guess right. She thought it must be some busybody inspector-of-something-or-other. Giving her a polite, mechanical smile she went on milking, waiting for an explanation.

'I'm sorry I was foul to you last night,' the woman said.

Jinny was so startled that she nearly kicked the bucket over. There was no mistaking that deep, clear voice. 'You're —'

'No, don't stop milking.' Harriet Shakespeare waved an impatient hand. 'I expect you've got to finish it before you can do anything else.'

She took off her glasses and turned down the collar. Her pudgy face was very pale and her eyes looked as bad as Jinny's felt. She knew it, too. As she ran a hand over her short hair, she pulled a face.

'I must look like death. But I've been up all night. You can imagine. I was on to the exchange for your name and number as soon as the news came through, but it took me an hour and a half to bully someone into looking up where the phone-box was. And ever since then, more or less, I've been driving. I had to knock up the girl in the Post Office to find out where you lived and — here I am. I feel like a warmed up corpse, but I wanted to get to you before the police thought of it. Or before you went to them again.'

She tapped the arm of her glasses against her teeth and watched Jinny with sharp, pale blue eyes. In an odd way she seemed too solid, too highly coloured. More real than other people because her face was so familiar, although she was a stranger.

And totally incomprehensible. 'I'm sorry,' Jinny said, 'but I don't understand. Have you changed your mind since last night?'

'You don't know?' Eyebrows rose above the blue eyes and the pale, squashed face frowned, with impatience very close below the surface. 'You haven't heard any *News*?'

Jinny stood up and lifted one of the buckets. Immediately,

139

Harriet Shakespeare picked up the other and followed her out to the trough, talking all the time.

'Look — it's hard to explain clearly when you're shattered but yesterday I thought you were a ghoul. Having me on. Or a crank. I *knew* where Liam was. Then, last night, I discovered I was wrong.'

Copying Jinny's example, she hoisted the bucket into the trough. Then she bent over and, with a flick of her hand splashed cold water and smoothed it over her face.

'That's better. Dammit, if only I could keep *awake*.' She caught at Jinny's wrist. 'I came to find you because you were the only person who *told* me that Liam wouldn't be in that house. You're my only hope. Where is he? How do I get him out?'

Her fingers tightened, bending the wrist back painfully, and at last Jinny understood. She had spent so many hours last night thinking about a pathetic, grief-stricken Harriet Shakespeare that this small, tough woman had taken her by surprise, almost annoyed her. But she was just as desperate, as grief-stricken as Jinny had imagined. Not pathetic, but certainly panicking.

At least I can deal with that, thought Jinny. *The Imogen Slattery special. Calming people down.* She took a deep breath and made herself speak slowly.

'Look, I can show you where he is if you like. But there's no use in that. You can't just knock on the door and ask for him. We need to sit down and talk about what to do.'

The fingers on her wrist squeezed harder.

'Don't you understand? There's almost no time left. We can't lounge about chatting.'

'But I thought we had until Friday,' Jinny said, puzzled. 'The newspapers said the deadline was Friday.'

'Oh *That*!' Harriet Shakespeare brushed the idea away. 'That's a decoy. The real deadline is today. At two o'clock.'

Aha, thought Jinny. *There's one up for you, Keith. She has got a secret.* And then she almost panicked herself. Seven hours. Only seven hours. And suppose she was wrong, after all? She swallowed.

'What — what's got to be done by two o'clock? What's the ransom? Not all that Community Home business by the Government?'

'That? No. That is — ' Harriet Shakespeare wavered. Stopped and shook her head as though to clear it. The action seemed to calm her slightly, and when she spoke again her voice had dropped half a tone. 'Look, I haven't got to do anything by two o'clock except get Liam out. So *please* let's find somewhere we can sit down and make a plan.'

'I'll just turn the cow out,' Jinny muttered. She wanted a few moments to think. Wrenching her wrist free, she walked back to the milking house with her mind a complete blank.

And then, miraculously, through the gap in the out-buildings, she saw a familiar, reassuring figure galloping up the track, with his clothes all huddled on anyhow and his hair unbrushed. Jinny waved frantically.

'Keith!'

He burst into the yard, tripped over a duck and nearly fell over.

'Jinny! Rachel's got the most peculiar story — '

Then he saw the figure standing by the water trough and his voice faded away, with an apologetic, lop-sided grin.

'Oh,' he said softly. 'So Rachel was right. I thought she was teasing me.'

Jinny turned back to Harriet Shakespeare. 'This is my friend Keith Hollins. The brother of the girl you spoke to at the Post Office.' With Keith behind her, she felt much more confident and determined and she held out a hand to each of them. 'We'll go indoors. There's always breakfast and Planning here at this time. Looks like all of us could do with a bit of both.'

She led them towards the kitchen, certain that Bella would make them welcome and throw another three or four collops of bacon into the pan.

Incredibly, it was not until she pushed open the kitchen

door that she remembered just what day it was and what they were all supposed to be doing.

7.15 a.m.

Very carefully, without looking right or left, Tug punctured the top of his egg with his fork. Then he speared a square of fried bread and dipped it in, turning it about until it was yellow all over. Very carefully, concentrating on what he was doing.

Now, he asked himself as he chewed the bread, *do I always do it like that?* He fixed his mind deliberately on the question, not letting it wander. Yes, he probably did. He liked to eat methodically and tidily, not picking and leaving bits on his plate. Eating was part of the serious business of training your body and keeping it fit. Still, he could not be *quite* sure that he always did that with his bread. Not sure enough to write it on his precious list.

Still staring down, he began to cut another square of bread. Neatly. Forcing himself not to think about anything else.

It was not really any use. All the time, whatever he did, he was aware of Doyle and the Woman. They sat one on either side of him, at the ends of the table, each with a cup of coffee and a half-eaten slice of toast. Doyle was frowning down at yesterday's paper, pretending to do the crossword. He liked to finish it each morning before he fetched the new day's papers. But today he was only doodling in the margin, leaving the black and white diagram empty. The Woman was gazing out of the window, picking at the hem of the table-cloth. They were both jumpy and alert. Their guns were on the table by their hands, out of Tug's reach, and from both of them came a feeling of expectant tension.

Ever since Tug opened his eyes and saw Doyle in front of the door, things had been different from the other mornings.

142

Doyle had barked at him. Ordered him out of bed and impatiently interrupted his exercises to bring him downstairs for breakfast. Normally they ate late and Tug was kept in the attic. But today it was as though Doyle and the Woman needed to be together, even though they were not talking. Today was not like any other day of his captivity, and Tug was afraid of it.

Which was why he dipped the second piece of fried bread carefully in the egg and turned it about, concentrating on making it yellow all over.

'If you don't stop playing with your food, I'll take it away,' Doyle said quietly. 'If I have to watch you any longer I'll throw up all over the table.'

'Sorry.' Tug thrust the bread into his mouth and began to eat faster.

But it seemed that he had sparked something off. Doyle looked from him to the Woman and back again and his face twisted into an expression of complete scorn. 'What a way to spend a day! Watching a kid fiddling around with fried bread. What sort of life is that?'

'Doyle — ' said the Woman.

'Shut up!' Doyle turned to Tug and his eyes narrowed. 'Are you really contented? Just sitting there and pushing food into your face? Suppose you knew that this was going to be the last day of your life. What would you choose to be doing?'

'*Doyle!*' The Woman glared at him and put her hand on Tug's arm. 'He doesn't mean what you think. It's a question we all got — that always gets asked when — '

'Quiet.' Doyle did not raise his voice, but it silenced her. He had not even looked towards her again. He was watching Tug steadily, almost unblinking. 'Come on,' he said softly. 'If you don't know what you'd choose to do on the last day of your life, you don't know what's really important to you. What matters when parents stop pushing and other people's eyes stop looking and you're alone with yourself. No one else to be afraid of. No one else to please.' His voice was low, but he was breathing harder and his eyes gleamed as though he

143

held Tug in a trap. 'Only free people know the answer to that question.'

Did he mean free people or Free People? Tug blinked at him.

'Come on,' crooned Doyle.

The Woman suddenly sat up straighter. 'We both did it once. For a test. We faced the barrel of a gun and chose the last thing we would do. *I* said I would drive into the country, lie in the long grass and watch the sun go down until it was quite dark. But I was wrong. It wasn't enough. Not for the last day of my life. It wasn't what I really wanted.'

Doyle's eyes slid towards her contemptuously. 'Of course it wasn't. Only a sentimental, middle-class idiot would have thought of it. Sunset!'

'What about you?' Tug said. He did not really understand the conversation, but he knew that the Woman was being attacked. Turning the attack back on Doyle was a way of defending her — and of putting off the moment when he had to answer the question himself. 'What would *you* do?'

Doyle's mouth curved upwards as though he were smiling, but with no humour. '*I* said I would gather together everything connected with my father — every photograph, every piece of clothing, his books, his certificates, his stamp collection — everything. I made a great bonfire of it and stood and watched it burn until every trace of him was wiped off the face of the earth.'

'And?' murmured the Woman. 'Was *that* enough?'

For a second the icy eyes were distant, remembering something pleasurable. Then they snapped back to attention and Doyle shook his head. 'No. It was very good, but it wasn't good enough.'

'So you see,' the Woman said to Tug, 'it's not easy to know what you want. Because to do that, you have to know who you *are*. Who you *really* are. And how many people can be sure of things about themselves when they've been brought up to please other people? Forced into jobs they don't like. Trained to conform to the million tiny rules that each family makes for itself.'

144

'You think you're Liam Shakespeare,' Doyle said softly. '*We* say you're Philip Doyle. Without one name or the other, you're lost. You don't know how to be a person without a family to prop you up. And you can't answer my question, can you? You don't know who you are!'

They were both staring at him. Fierce eyes. *Mad eyes,* thought Tug. *Mad questions. Why should I play their games?* and yet—he slid his hand into his pocket and fingered the folded sheets of paper, hastily bundled together.

'Yes I *do* know who I am.' His voice came out perfectly steady, not defiant, but certain. It was obvious from the way the staring eyes blinked, both pairs together, that they had not been expecting an answer. Not any answer. Tug brushed his thumb along the edge of the paper and thought of everything that was written on it. The food he liked. The things he could do. His pulse rate and the number of his teeth and his daily exercise plan. His secret fears and his even more secret hopes.

'Well?' said Doyle. 'If you're so sure, what would *you* do on the last day of your life?'

Tug gazed out of the window at the mist lying in the bottom of the dale and the indistinct grey ridges stretching away from the cottage. What could he do that would sum up everything he knew about himself? What would satisfy every part of him — body and mind and will? What would use all his feelings and skills and understanding? For a whole minute he stared out of the window and wondered.

And then he knew the answer. It came into his head, clear and beautiful and complete. Standing up, he gazed through the window at the massive gritstone ridge which stood against the sky on the other side of the main dale. It ran, high and level and almost straight, from the north, where its precipitous crags dropped sheer from the edge, black against the pale, early morning light, to the south, where a jagged lump stood up, breaking its smooth run.

'What's that?' he said. 'That long hill?'

Doyle smiled, with sneering triumph, thinking he had given

145

up. 'That's Ashdale Great Edge. The *famous* local feature that families come miles to gawp at. On their lovely family holidays. And the lump at the far end is the Castle Rock.'

Tug took a calm, deep breath. 'I can tell you what I'd do on the last day of my life,' he said. 'I'd run.' He could almost feel the hard unevenness of the ground under his feet as he spoke. 'I'd run the length of Ashdale Great Edge, from this end to the Castle Rock, as fast as I could.'

'Another idyllic, bourgeois idea,' Doyle said sarcastically.

Tug shook his head. He was remembering the strength that came gloriously from nowhere when your body seemed to be finished. The triumphant feeling that it was impossible to try any harder. That was what he wanted. Not people to applaud him. Not a beautiful picture of himself running into the sunset. Not even a world-beating time. Just to run to the end of his endurance — and then to go on. Once more. *That's what I'd do*, he thought. *I know that's what I want, and no one can take that away from me. Whoever I am.*

'Finish your breakfast, Tug,' the Woman said. 'It's getting cold.'

As he sat down, he looked sideways at her. He wanted her to understand that the running was not just a pretty fancy, that he had been serious. Somehow, whatever she was to him, it was important for her to believe that. But her face startled him. She was staring at him, with her great golden eyes, and her expression was so sad and apprehensive that the sight of it shocked him into asking the question he had been trying to ignore. The question that had lurked under the surface of the whole conversation.

'So — is this going to be the last day of my life?'

It was Doyle who answered, thoughtfully, as though it had been any ordinary question.

'I think perhaps — not. It will be the last day of someone's life, but not yours, I think.'

Joe Slattery flicked his long, straight hair back behind his ears and rubbed his chin.

'Oz,' Bella said, 'go and let the chickens out. Then walk down to Far Field and wait. If people start arriving, tell them Joe's on his way.'

Oz stuck out his bottom lip. 'I want to stay and — '

'Oz,' Joe interrupted, 'this is the only day in the year when I need to ask for help from my neighbours. I *will* have them treated politely.' His voice was low, but Oz slid off his chair immediately and made for the door. 'And Oz—not a word, eh?'

Glancing over his shoulder with a huge wink, Oz banged the door after him and went whooping across the yard. Joe looked down at the table.

'Let me get this straight, Mrs Shakespeare,' he said slowly. 'This boy — who you *think* is your son — is staying up in Back Clough Dale with a couple who may — or may not — be armed terrorists. You don't want to go to the police, because you're afraid they'll simply get involved in another siege — *if* you can make them believe you in time, which seems doubtful. So you want me to help you to produce a plan to solve the whole thing in the next five or six hours. On harvest day.'

'Yes,' said Harriet Shakespeare.

She had not eaten or drunk anything since she walked in. She had not even spoken much, leaving the explanations to Keith and Jinny. She had just sat still, next to Bella, and stared at Joe, with fierce, desperate eyes.

Joe tapped his fingertips together and looked from face to face. 'Do they ever go out, these Doyle people?' he said abruptly.

'I've not seen them out all together.' It was Keith who answered, stumbling over the words because he was so eager to help. 'One of the—the adults turns up at the shop every day, I think. Mam said they'd ordered *two* daily

147

papers, and they must come down to collect those.'

Joe gazed at the ceiling and tapped his fingers for a little longer. Then he sat up straight.

'The plan's simple,' he said briskly. 'You'll never get that boy out of the house. Not if everyone in the village joins in an attack. It's too easy for the others to put a gun to his head.'

In Back Clough Dale? thought Jinny. Then she imagined the Hare-woman with a gun in her hand — and changed her mind. The picture was easy to make. Too easy.

'So,' Joe continued, 'we've got to lure the others out and lock the boy *in*. That will give us a breathing space to sort things out. And if it's all a mistake, there'll be no harm done and no shooting. Cottage door's got a bolt, hasn't it, Keith?'

Keith hesitated and the rest of them watched him anxiously, holding their breath.

'Ye — es,' he said. Then 'Oh yes. Now I remember. There's two. Top and bottom.'

'Right,' said Joe. 'This is how it would work. A couple of you get down there as fast as you can and watch the cottage. As soon as one of the adults goes for the paper, we'll send in a Trojan Horse. Have to be Jinny, I think. She's the only one who's small enough not to worry anyone.'

Bella opened her mouth to disagree, glanced at Harriet Shakespeare and shut it again.

'Jinny gets inside the cottage with some excuse or other,' Joe waved his hand, not bothering about details. 'Meanwhile, the other watcher races down to Far Field and tells me. I'll come up with two or three of the other men and knock on the door. We should have fifteen or twenty minutes clear before the other Doyle gets back. As soon as the door's opened, we grab the person who opens it and haul him outside. Or her. Only got to do it for a second. Just long enough for Jinny to bolt the door. Then we ask our questions.'

'Suppose I can't get in?' Jinny said.

'Still no harm done.' Joe shrugged. 'They're not going to shoot you just for trying. We'll have to make other plans, that's all.'

148

'Who goes with Jinny? To watch?' said Keith.

Joe nodded. 'You, of course. Mrs Shakespeare can go too, if she likes, *but she must not be seen*. This plan's only going to be successful if they don't suspect anything, and if they see her around they'll suspect lots. Got any more questions?'

Nobody spoke for a second. Then Harriet Shakespeare said briskly, 'It's a good plan. The best we're going to get. Keith, Jinny — are you coming?'

She had begun to push back her chair when Joe spoke suddenly.

'Wait. *I* have a question.'

He was very pale. As everyone turned to look at him, Jinny realized that he had been waiting for this moment all the time he was explaining his plan. She had been surprised when he seemed to join in so easily. She knew how much he hated relying on other people or being involved in their affairs. Now she saw that he had just been dealing with the easy, practical part first. Before he got to the real problem.

Harriet Shakespeare caught the idea as well. She went as pale as he was and clenched her fists.

'What question?'

'The most basic question of all,' murmured Joe. '*Why*? We're racing round and cobbling up a makeshift plan. On the most inconvenient day of the whole year for me. You want me to disrupt my harvest and put my daughter in danger — and yet, according to Keith, the terrorists in your house were saying that their deadline was Friday. It's only Tuesday today. Why the desperate hurry?'

'I *told* you,' Harriet Shakespeare said. 'The real deadline *is* today. At two o'clock.'

Joe shook his head. 'That's nonsense. People don't bring deadlines *closer*. Not unless they're sure of getting what they have demanded.'

'Or unless those demands are a blind,' said Keith. He had sat almost silently up till then, but his face was intent. 'Free People like to play mind games, don't they? What if they're using the *public* demands and the *public*

149

deadline to distract attention from—something else?'

'Oh what a genius you are,' Harriet Shakespeare said wearily. 'Yes, of course you're right. The siege has given them publicity for their ideas, of course, but what they *really* want, to save Liam's life, is something quite different. Only I know what that is — and that's all I can say.'

'That's not good enough.' Joe was relentless. 'I *have* to know what you're being asked for. Why should I put myself to a lot of trouble and difficulty when — perhaps — you could just give the terrorists what they ask and save all the bother?'

'But if I tell you,' Harriet Shakespeare said, as though she were talking to an idiot, 'I'm putting Liam's life in worse danger. Just by telling you.'

Joe did not even hesitate. 'You're asking me to put *my daughter* in danger. My first duty is to my family.'

Suddenly, startlingly, Harriet Shakespeare's mouth twisted. She gave a loud, bitter shout of laughter that made them all stare. Then she sat, very straight-backed, and looked hard at Joe.

'Listen, then. Understand what Free People have been doing to me. They're not like any other group I've ever investigated. They're clever and devious and dramatic. Oh, they're as violent as any other terrorists, and they like to shock. But they like to puzzle and tease and make people *think*, as well. Playing mind games, like Keith said.'

'A siege that's not a siege in London,' murmured Keith. 'A family that's not a family in Derbyshire. A fake siege hiding a kidnapping and fake demands that camouflage something else.'

Harriet Shakespeare nodded. 'You're getting the idea. But you haven't seen how all this ties in with their long-term aims. You haven't seen the moral. They want to turn people against the family as a system. Because—oh, I guess you know most of the reasons already.' She had been talking very fast, as though it made her impatient to explain. But suddenly her voice slowed and she looked down at her

150

hands. 'If you were Free People and you wanted to strike a shocking, symbolic blow at the family—something that everyone in the country would feel—which family would you bomb?'

Bella got it first. She gasped. 'But that's *impossible*. What about security?'

'It only takes one fanatic,' Harriet Shakespeare said heavily. 'A fanatic with a bomb in the right crowd at the right time. At two o'clock this afternoon.'

'He'd *need* to be a fanatic,' Keith said grimly. 'It could be the end of *his* life as well.'

'But that's another of their little games,' said Harriet Shakespeare. Her voice was stretched very tight, as though it might snap at any moment and tumble her into tears. 'To get into the group at all, you have to say what you'd do if you knew you were going to die tomorrow. And then they make you do it — with a gun pointed at the back of your neck. You don't find out that the gun's not loaded until *after* you've heard the trigger click. They're used to the idea of dying, you see.' -

'You know a lot about them.' Jinny ran a finger along the edge of the table. 'You must have spent ages investigating.' She could see the whole thing now, crystal-clear. 'And when you found out about this new plan of theirs, they kidnapped Liam to stop you telling.'

'*Oh!*' Impulsively, Bella put a warm, soft arm round Harriet Shakespeare's shoulders, but the shoulders did not droop. They stayed rigid and determined, like their owner's voice.

'It's a very pretty problem, isn't it?' she said. 'If I tell — they will kill Liam and point out that he's had to suffer for my stubborn principles. And that's what being in a family does for you. If I *don't* tell,' she gripped the edge of the table, 'there will be several deaths this afternoon, less important to me, but much more sensational. And Free People will be able to announce that being in a family is corrupting. That my love for my son has interfered with my passion for truth and

151

justice. The passion that I have foolishly boasted so much about. Very neat. Either way, Free People get their moral. And lots of free publicity.' She put her head in her hands and sat very still.

It was Keith who spoke first, looking red-faced and embarrassed. 'I don't want to sound awkward, but — you said Free People were devious. Don't you think it might be a hoax? No bomb, no fanatic. Just a trick to find out what you would do? That way they still get their moral.'

'Don't you think I've been trying to believe that?' Harriet Shakespeare said thickly. 'That would let me nicely off the hook. And it's the sort of thing they could do. Just like their initiation ceremony. But—they *have* got bombs. We know that. And — have I got the right to take the risk?'

She looked up and her face was only just under control, balanced on the edge of screaming. *It's always the people you love who trap you like that.* Jinny remembered Bella's words and understood them properly for the first time. How could Harriet Shakespeare choose what to do — how could she face making the choice — when her own son was involved?

Joe stood up and came down the table towards Harriet Shakespeare. 'It's all right,' he said, looking down at her bent back. 'I understand now. There's nothing you can do except stand up for your own and try and get Liam out before two o'clock. We'll just have to pray it's him in there.'

At last she raised her head. 'You'll help, then?'

Joe did not answer directly. Instead, he looked across the table. 'I haven't got the most dangerous part. What about you, Jinny? Will you do it?'

'Oh, of *course*.' She jumped up. It would be such a relief to be doing something practical, after all this talk. 'Let's get up there quickly and start watching. I'm *sure* we can do it. Are you coming, Mrs Shakespeare?'

Harriet Shakespeare stood up. 'Yes. I know I can't help, but just to be *there* will make me feel I'm fighting to get Liam back. Better than dripping around here.'

They were half-way to the door before Jinny realized that

152

the third person was missing. She turned and saw him still sitting at the table. 'Keith?'

His face was heavy and miserable. 'Look — I don't want to blight the whole thing before we start, but — suppose we fail? Suppose it's *not* Liam in there? We've *got* to do something about the bomb before we start. Tell Dad or something, so the police know. I don't think — ' he looked even more distressed ' — that it's fair to gamble with people's lives.'

'What about Liam's life — ?' began Jinny. But Harriet Shakespeare put a finger on her wrist to stop her. Then she looked at Keith, every muscle in her face drawn tight.

'Do you think I haven't been over every *inch* of that argument a million times? And you're right. Of course. I had to change my mind.' She gulped for breath, as though she could hardly bear what she was saying. 'Yesterday I phoned the police and now, if we don't get Liam out by two o'clock, he'll die for certain.'

11.00 a.m.

The Woman shut the door and turned the key in the lock. From outside came the noise of Doyle starting the car. All morning he had been in a strange, erratic mood and as the car began to bump its way off down the track Tug felt a great lightening of his spirits.

'Whee!' he said softly.

The Woman turned and, for a second, he saw a reflection of the same feeling on her face. They grinned at each other like conspirators.

'Ma — '

Her smile vanished. 'Come on. He'll be back soon. How about getting the breakfast cleared up?'

Tug started to stack the dirty plates. 'I was better off when

153

I was eating upstairs, wasn't I? Waited on hand and foot up there. Down here I'm a slave.'

He leaned across the table to reach the last cup and suddenly froze. There, lying on the Woman's chair, where she had left it, was her gun. The long Kalashnikov. Within his grasp. For a moment his fingers trembled, hovering over it, and then he gripped it firmly with both hands. When he looked up, the Woman was watching him.

'Well?' she said quietly. 'Doyle was right. I *am* careless with that gun. You can shoot me now, can't you? And then escape.'

Tug made the pictures in his head. Aiming. No need to be particularly careful at such short range. A jerk of the finger on the trigger. He had a feeling there would be something complicated about a safety catch, but he might be able to work it out. A burst of gun-fire and then — what? He would have to heave her blood-stained body away from the door and then scramble over it before he could race out and lose himself in the hills.

Somehow the pictures were not quite real enough. They were story-book pictures. Holding the gun very still and steady, pointed at her, he said, 'Could *you* shoot *me*? Really, I mean?'

She did not answer at once, but she went very pale. As she hesitated, Tug found that he desperately wanted to know what she would say. He stared hard at her face as, at last, her lips began to move.

'I — '

Then came the knock on the door.

Both of them stopped, stiffening, and the Woman glanced sharply at Tug.

'Don't mind me.' Gently he put the gun down on the table and carried the pile of plates over to the sink. 'I'm just the kitchen-maid round here.' But his blood seemed to be flowing at twice the normal speed and he stood carefully, so that he could see the doorway.

The Woman slipped Doyle's gun into her bag and slid the

154

Kalashnikov under a cushion. Then she turned the key, slowly and quietly, and opened the door.

'Hallo,' said a familiar voice, a little fast and breathless. 'My Dad sent me up here. He said we owed you a favour, because of all that fuss and bother about the dog that was chasing sheep. He doesn't like to owe things.'

It was the girl who had come with the policeman. She looked very small and slight standing there with her skinny plait and her pale, freckled face. Disappointed, Tug turned back to the sink, listening vaguely to what she said as he began to wash up.

'I'm *sorry* about the dog thing. We'd like to ask you all down to the Harvest, to make up. Oh — that must sound funny to you. As if we're asking you to do our work. It's not like that. There's so many folk it's more like a party. With lots of beer and home-made bread and cheese and ham and some of my mother's special cakes and — '

'What a pity,' interrupted the Woman. 'You've just missed my husband. How funny you didn't see him.' Tug heard the suspicion in her voice, but it did not seem to worry the girl.

'I must confess,' she said cheerily. 'I waited till he was gone. He scares me stupid.'

'Well, we'll have to consult him,' said the Woman. But she sounded amused now. Amused and relaxed.

'Oh, *do* come!' Suddenly, the girl darted past her, into the kitchen, and ran across to the sink, catching at Tug's sleeve.

'Philip, do persuade her. It's real fun. *Special!*'

Tug was so surprised that he dropped the cloth he was holding. She had grabbed his arm, hard enough to bruise it, and she was staring wildly at him, as though she meant something quite different.

But before he could answer her, there was a noise outside. A car was coming up the track at high speed, creaking and groaning as it went over the bumps. The Woman looked out.

'Doyle's back,' she said, sounding puzzled.

Tug had just one glimpse of the girl's horror as her mouth and her eyes opened wide. The next moment she had her face

155

under control, turning towards the door with a polite smile.

The car-door slammed. Feet raced across the yard, scattering gravel, and Doyle burst through the door. He was breathless and moving at high speed, but there was nothing agitated or uncontrolled about him. He had begun to give orders before he was properly inside.

'Come on!' he yelled at the Woman. 'And bring the boy. We've got to get out of here. Harriet Shakespeare's around!'

'*What?*' said the Woman.

Tug caught his breath and his head spun. Hank! But was it Hank? But there was no time to think about that. Doyle had seen the girl.

'Bring her too!' he snapped. 'And the guns. And the *radio.*'

Then they were being hustled towards the car. It had only two doors and by the time they had been pushed roughly into the back, with the Woman leaning round in the front seat to point the small gun at them, they hardly dared to breathe.

The Woman was pale. Her eyes seemed to have grown even larger and they stared grimly at Tug and the girl, barely blinking as she watched every movement. It seemed incredible to Tug that only five minutes before he had been calling her Ma and they had been grinning at each other.

'So — how did you find out?' she said to Doyle, without turning her head. 'Did you see her?'

'No. I picked up that silly, mincing girl from the Post Office. She was walking that way, and I could hardly ignore her. Natural chatterer. All the gossip.' He imitated a shrill, foolish voice and Tug could tell that it was a good imitation because the girl next to him looked up sharply. 'You'll never *guess* who knocked on our door this morning . At *half past six!* It gave me a real *shock* to see her. It was *Harriet Shakespeare!*'

It must *mean something that she was here*, thought Tug. But he had stopped trusting his thoughts.

The Woman smiled dryly. 'So you pushed her out of the car and gave the whole game away?'

'Think I'm a fool?' Doyle said scornfully. 'I said I'd

forgotten my wallet. Dropped her off and came screeching back here.'

He was driving even faster now. Tug looked into the barrel of the gun and prayed. Gradually everything else faded out of his mind. All he could think of was the small, dark, murderous hole. *Please don't let it go off by accident. Please don't let her finger jerk by mistake.* He was more frightened than he had been in all the time he had been with them, and he could tell that the girl was frightened too, by her quick, shallow breathing.

'So you came crashing in,' the Woman said, still sounding unimpressed. 'Saddled us with another kid and raced off without any plan.'

'Don't you understand?' Doyle shouted. 'That place was a trap once they knew we were there. No proper view round and only one exit. We need somewhere safe to sit out the last two or three hours.'

'So you *have* got a plan?'

'Of course I've got a plan, and you'll see what it is in a few moments, if you're too stupid to guess before that — ' They swung round a bend and he swore suddenly and loudly.

Tug had a sharp, split-second picture of people walking on the track. Three or four men. He had never seen any of them before, but the girl knocked on the window and shouted to them.

'Shut up!' With a single, sharp blow, the Woman knocked her sideways, into Tug's lap.

Doyle put his foot down and drove straight at the men. There was a terrifying moment of confusion when faces loomed round the windows, voices bellowed and hands banged and battered at the roof of the car. But the men gave way, because they had no choice, and the next minute the car had bounced out on to the road, turning left, away from the village and up towards the dale head.

'*Oh!*' said the Woman suddenly.

She's guessed where we're going, thought Tug. But he could not guess himself. His mind seemed to have gone into a

157

paralysing panic. All he could take in was the muzzle of the gun, the silent terror of the girl next to him and the Woman's stony face.

The car climbed the steep, twisting road at brake-squealing speed, until it reached the crest, where the fields stopped and the open moor began. Doyle swerved, running the car on to the right hand verge, and braked hard. Then he snatched the gun from the Woman's hand, opened the car door and slid out, tilting his seat forward.

'Out, you two!'

Tug and the girl slithered out and Doyle jerked the gun towards the narrow squeeze-stile in the drystone wall beside them.

'Get going.' Edging between the two tall, upright stones, Tug heard him mutter at the Woman, 'Lock up the car and bring the Kalashnikov. *And the radio.*' Then, louder, 'Go on, you kids. Get walking. And don't forget there's a gun behind you.'

'But — we can't get anywhere this way,' the girl said.

'Shut up! Walk!'

They stepped out across the moorland and the wind caught them, strong and cold, once they were out of the shelter of the wall. Tug looked sideways, towards the valley on the right, and recognized where they were. They were walking on to the long ridge they had been able to see from the cottage window. Ashdale Great Edge. And he had the strange feeling that he was moving in a dream. Past and future were wiped out, and there was nothing real except the wind on his face and the springy heather and the small, tough bushes under his feet. Beside him, the girl walked at the same pace, just out of step with him. Like a person who walks beside you in a dream, she did not speak except once. Then, in a strange, high voice, she said, 'The Edge is good for bilberries.'

'Good for wind too,' said Tug. And his voice sounded high and strange as well.

They walked like robots until Doyle yelled, 'Stop!' with half his voice whirled away by the wind so that it came to them as a little thread of sound. They had just reached the path that ran the length of the Edge, the barren ridge stretching in front of them, flat and clear all the way to the Castle Rock. On their left it sloped gently away and on the right it fell sheer, in steep crags. They had an uninterrupted view of all the directions in which people might approach.

'What now?' said the Woman. 'End of the world?'

Doyle did not waste time smiling. 'We watch for visitors.'

They did not have long to wait. It was only a moment or two before a couple of cars came up the hill and screeched into the side of the road. Tug watched the people get out. The three or four men that Doyle had driven at, a tall, ungainly boy of about eighteen — and Hank.

But he was still in the remote coldness of his dream. As he watched her squeeze through the stile and walk forward with the others, she seemed strange and unreal, like something he had imagined when he was a very little boy. So much had happened since he last saw her.

Doyle let the little group of people walk on until it was only about two hundred metres away. Then he caught hold of the girl, roughly, by her plait, and dragged her round in front of him. With a deliberate, unmistakable gesture, he put the gun to her head.

'Stay there!' he yelled, at the top of his voice.

The wind blew his words at the men and they stopped, glancing at each other. Doyle did not let go of the girl's plait, but he jerked at it, to make her sit down.

'And now?' said the Woman.

Doyle smiled, almost beautifully, as though everything had come right, and handed her the small gun. 'Keep guard. I'm going to put on the radio.' He squatted down and propped it against a clump of little bushes, pulling up the aerial as far as it would go. Then he fiddled with the controls until he had produced a clear sound that was audible even over the wind. He glanced over his shoulder at the crowd of people. They were still standing two hundred metres away, afraid to come any nearer, and he smiled. 'Sit down everyone,' he said softly.

159

'There's plenty of time. We're going to wait and listen to the News.'

Of course, thought Tug. *Why not?* In its frosty, stunned isolation, his mind found it quite natural to be out in the wind in this remote place, waiting for a disembodied voice. He sat cross-legged on the ground and stared into the black grid on the front of the radio.

2.25 p.m.

The wind was blowing over the top of Jinny's head, fluttering the loose, short hairs round her forehead.

It's an important wind, she thought dully. *It'll probably be the last wind I shall ever feel. I should be enjoying it.* But she could not make herself care.

When she knocked on the door of Back Clough Dale Cottage, she had been afraid but in control. That was less than three and a half hours ago, but it might have been years. It might have been a different person. Ever since Doyle burst through the door, furious and shouting and shoving, she had stiffened into ice. She did not *feel* afraid, but when she looked down at her hands she saw that they were shaking.

Her moment of complete despair had come when Doyle switched on the radio and sat down to wait and see what happened. *We're waiting to hear the News.* And only Jinny knew that the news he wanted would never come. Could not come. She sat and stared along the Edge, down into the dale, not bothering to strain her ears and listen to the radio, because she knew it was pointless. Not looking back the way they had come, because she could not bear to watch Joe. She imagined him haggard and afraid, even though she was too far away to see his face clearly. People had come and gone in the little crowd. The blue uniforms of policemen had appeared and marksmen had fanned out, hunting for good positions to aim from. But no one was any nearer. Every time anyone made a threatening move, the Hare-woman hauled

160

Jinny to her feet and pointed the gun at her head until the person gave way and retreated. And always she and Doyle made sure that their bodies were shielded by the other two. The worst thing of all was that no one was talking. Jinny had made one attempt to say something to the boy, but Doyle stopped her immediately, catching hold of her chin and jerking her head away. Now they sat avoiding each other's eyes.

Jinny avoided the Hare-woman's eyes too. It was almost unbearable to look into them. All the time those steady, golden eyes had fascinated her — and now they were looking steadily at her along the barrel of a gun. If she moved, the Hare-woman would kill her. And the terrible, disturbing thing was that there was nothing different. It was just this power and seriousness that had fascinated her in the first place.

'Listen!' said Doyle suddenly.

His voice was quiet, but the effect, after their long silence, was as though he had shouted. The other three swivelled round to look at him.

'Listen carefully to this News,' he said, with no expression in his face. 'All of you, but especially Tug. This is the one that really matters. We're waiting to hear of deaths. Of certain important deaths that were due to occur at two o'clock. If the news comes, all your worries are over.'

'And if not?' the boy said, almost defiantly.

'If not,' murmured Doyle, 'you will know that Harriet Shakespeare has chosen to save those important lives — instead of saving her son's. Presumably because *he* is less important.'

Not true, Jinny wanted to say, watching the boy's face go white. *It's not like that at all. I've seen how much she loves you.*

But she dared not say anything. Instead, she crouched over the radio, listening, like all the others, as the news bulletin began.

Riots in a South American country.

Reports that the economy might improve in six months' time.

Cross-channel ferries held up by a bomb scare . . . .

It was too late already. They all knew it. Important deaths come in special news flashes, or as the first item, not at the end. If the deaths had taken place, they would know it by now. But Doyle listened right to the last word of the News. Right up to the moment when the news-reader said, 'And that's the end of the News. The next News will be at — '

Then he switched off.

'Now,' he said, 'we talk.'

'What is there to talk about?' said the boy, still in that funny, cold, high-pitched voice. 'You're going to kill me, aren't you?'

Jinny clenched her fists, digging the nails into the palms of her hands. But no one looked at her. Doyle and the Hare-woman were both staring at the boy. Doyle nodded.

'Oh, we're going to kill you all right. Don't start kidding yourself that there's any way out of that. But first — you've got a choice to make. The last one you'll ever have, and the most significant.'

He was speaking very slowly and clearly, as if he wanted to make sure that the boy understood. Now he gestured backwards, towards the group by the wall.

'Harriet Shakespeare's over there. I can't imagine what brought her, but I'm certain you've seen her.'

'*I* brought her,' Jinny interrupted frantically. 'I telephoned her and said I was sure he — Philip — was Liam Shakespeare, and she came racing here from London.' She clutched at the boy's arm. 'Don't listen to them. Of *course* she loves you. She's desperate.'

Doyle smiled scornfully, as though she had somehow missed the point. But it was still the boy he spoke to. 'Of course she loves *Liam Shakespeare*. But she can't be sure you're Liam, can she Tug? She's too far away to see you properly. And until *she's* sure, you can't be absolutely sure yourself. Can you?'

162

His voice had dropped lower and lower, until he was almost whispering, and he let the last question hang in the silence. It sounded nonsense to Jinny, but she saw the boy's face go pale.

'This is what I'm going to do,' crooned Doyle, in the same, soft voice. 'I'm going to signal to Harriet Shakespeare to walk across here. Slowly, so that we can watch her face. So that we can wait for the moment when she sees you well enough to be sure whether you are Liam or not. The moment when her expression changes. One way or the other.'

'And then,' said the boy, his eyes on Doyle's face, 'then you'll shoot me. Whoever I am.'

'Oh, *I* shan't shoot you,' Doyle murmured lightly. 'Your mother will do that.'

Jinny did not understand, but the boy's head turned and he stared at the Hare-woman.

'Ma? You would really — ?'

Doyle laughed before he had even finished. 'You don't believe she would do it? Don't know her very well, do you? She hasn't got a very good record as a mother. They took her last baby away from her twelve years ago. It had five broken ribs and a cracked skull, and it was brain-damaged for life.'

Jinny felt her breath stop as her eyes swivelled automatically to look at the Hare-woman. She saw the long, strong face go deliberately stiff. *So that's what's chasing you*, she thought. But she could not speak. Neither could the boy. He went on staring at the Hare-woman.

'Not lucky with your mothers, are you, Tug?' Doyle said. 'Neither of them fits the picture of a *proper* mother.'

For a minute more, the boy went on gazing at the Hare-woman. At last he muttered stiffly, 'You told me I had a choice.'

'That's right,' said Doyle. 'It's very simple. You can do what I've described. Wait for the look on Harriet Shakespeare's face to tell you who you are. Wait meekly for her to put you in a box and label you — give you a face to shelter behind, whether it fits or not. Or — '

'Or?' whispered the boy. But Jinny could tell from his voice that he knew the answer already, and when Doyle replied it was with a nod.

'Exactly. Or you can dare to be alone with yourself. Dare to do the thing you chose as being the most important. To find out whether it really *is* important to you.'

'What we're offering you,' the Hare-woman said — and her voice was almost gentle — 'is a choice between knowing who other people *think* you are and knowing who you really are, inside yourself. You can have one of those things before you die. But not both.'

Suddenly Jinny was furiously, recklessly angry. The boy looked sick and white and terrified and the other two were staring at him almost without blinking, as though they were sucking out his life through his eyes.

'You're as bad as Harriet Shakespeare said you were!' she yelled. 'You don't care about people at all. You're just playing mind games!'

But she did not break that concentrated stare.

'It's not a game,' Doyle said calmly. 'Is it, Tug?'

The boy shook his head. Picking up the long gun, Doyle ran his finger along the barrel and then held it out to the Hare-woman. She dropped the other gun — the little one — into the pocket of her jacket and reached for the wooden grip of the Kalashnikov.

'There you are,' Doyle said. 'We're ready, Tug. Don't go thinking you can outrun the bullets. This gun's got a range of about three hundred metres and your mother's a very good shot. So there's no way out. Just the choice to make.'

The wind suddenly seemed to have grown much colder, striking so fiercely against Jinny's cheek that it numbed it. For a second there was no sound except the swish of that wind across the hillside.

'Well, Tug?' Doyle said.

Tug's first reaction was to look towards the Woman. She had hit him and fed him, shouted at him for being idle and

164

comforted him when he woke in the night and was afraid. If she was not his mother, she had still crammed a lot of mothering, good and bad, into the last few days. Could she really be going to kill him now?

'Ma — '

But there was no point in continuing. She stared at him with a stiff, expressionless face. For a moment he was horribly, surprisingly hurt, as though she had disowned him. Then he understood that she was not going to help him, because she wanted him to make the choice.

He glanced to his right, towards the distant mass of the Castle Rock. If he ran in that direction, would he be able to dodge? Briefly he imagined himself jinking and swerving, avoiding the bullets until he was out of range. Then his common sense took over. There was no shelter to make for, anywhere on the long, wide ridge, and the heather and the little bushes would tangle his feet and trip him as soon as he strayed from the straight path. There was no way to escape. He was going to die whatever happened. Thinking about anything else was just a way of avoiding the choice.

The choice. He let his eyes slip the other way, towards the little group of waiting people, hunting along the front line until he picked out Harriet Shakespeare. He was sure — or almost sure — that he wasn't mad. That she was Hank, and his mother. But she seemed small and remote and somehow two-dimensional, like a picture. It was not only space which separated them. It was the whole complicated, confusing tangle of his life with Ma and Doyle. He had grown without her. Now, even if she did say, 'You are my son,' what would that mean? She could not know the things he had discovered about himself in the last few days. To wait for her would be like walking backwards.

And yet — what kind of a monster would he be if he ran off in the opposite direction? If she *were* his mother, and he let himself be shot without giving her a last chance of looking into his eyes?

Into her little boy's eyes.

165

Her — little — boy.

Oh Hank! — and he knew, this time, that he was appealing to a part of his mind and not to another person at all — *What would you choose?*

Suddenly, without trying, he knew what the *real* Harriet Shakespeare would say. With a fierce look on her tough, plain face. *For Heaven's sake, Tug, do I have to decide everything for you? You've got to rely on yourself. Be a person of your own.*

The picture of her in his head was so clear that he actually smiled. Of course she was his mother! He knew it now, without question. He loved her and trusted her understanding — and that made the choice perfectly simple after all. He stood up.

'Ready,' he said.

Turning his back on Hank, he began to run away from her, along the path towards the Castle Rock.

Jinny jerked as though someone had pulled at her. That was the last thing she had expected. She did not understand what could have made the boy run off in the opposite direction. Nor did she understand the expression that leapt on to the Hare-woman's face, lighting her eyes with a fierce, proud joy.

All that was mysterious. What Jinny *could* understand was the slow, careful way the Hare-woman settled her hands round the long gun.

'You can't!' Jinny shouted. 'You *can't!*'

She would have rushed forward to knock the gun aside, but she was not fast enough. Doyle gripped her closely from behind, pinning her arms to her sides and holding her motionless.

'Wait!' he hissed. 'Wait and see what happens!'

Too fast! Too fast! thought Tug, willing himself to slow down. There was no point in going off like a stone from a catapult. He couldn't outrun the bullets. He would just sprint himself to a standstill in a couple of hundred metres. His fear screamed at him to bolt, but he forced his mind into action, to plan the run sensibly.

Ahead of him was the Castle Rock. Two miles away? Something like that. That was his finishing line. That was what he had to concentrate on. The wind was much more powerful than he had realized. Bracing his body against it, he battered forwards, with his head down, and it ate away at his strength. He was out of training, too. Exercises in a room were all very well, but they were no substitute for running every day.

Distantly, muffled by the wind, he heard shouts from behind, but he bullied himself to ignore them. Concentrate. *Concentrate*. Forget Ma. Forget Hank. Forget everything except the pace and the effort of keeping your feet pounding steadily, the effort of keeping your body moving forward towards the pain.

Jinny was screaming now. Flinging her voice into the wind in a last, desperate attempt to make the Hare-woman put down the gun.

'It's not fair! It's not *fair*! You both did this sort of test, I know you did. But no one shot *you*. You got away with it. How can you shoot Tug? He hasn't done anything to you. It's *wicked!* You're both crazy! All your ideas are mad and — '

Doyle's hand suddenly clamped over her mouth, cutting off her voice and nearly stopping her breath.

'Get on with it, you stupid cow,' he said harshly to the Hare-woman. 'Stop dithering about, or it'll be too late. They're coming.'

And, out of the corner of her eye, Jinny saw that it was true. Harriet Shakespeare and the policemen had begun to creep closer, ready to run as soon as the first shot was fired.

The Hare-woman's hands steadied the gun and she started to lift it, taking aim.

Tug was suffering already from the lack of training and the

stupid way he had begun the run. His breathing was frightful and the unrelenting ache in his legs grew harsher with every stride. He started to be afraid that he would have to slow down, even to walk. Had he really chosen this *pain* as the way to spend his last minutes? He must be mad! His legs thudded on and on, but the movement was mechanical, with no spirit in it. What was the point of dying with your lungs gasping for breath? What was the point of running to the Castle Rock anyway? What was the point of doing anything, when you were going to die?

Standing dumb and immobilized in Doyle's hands, Jinny felt the last grains of fight trickle out of her. All her thinking and watching and planning, from the first sound of the car on the track while she and Joe crouched by the netted gate to that last desperate shout that Doyle had cut short, all that worrying and puzzling had ended up like this. Any moment now, one burst of shooting would make Harriet Shakespeare childless and turn the Hare-woman into a murderess. And she was not strong enough to stop what was going to happen. All she could do was stand there, a passive witness. It was all going to end wrong after all.

Closing her eyes, she let her whole body droop, limp in Doyle's hands.

Then, with his legs like dough and his breath tearing out of his chest, Tug raised his head and saw the jagged, ungainly outline of the Castle Rock, sharp against the sky. Dimly, he knew that somewhere inside him was the power to reach it. Because that was what he had decided to do. Dragging the last remnants of his determination together, he fixed his eyes on the dark, looming rock and thought, *I will.*

And suddenly, like a miracle, the extra strength came to him, and he was *running*. Hundreds of metres up in the sky above Ashdale, he was running along the Edge with every last fibre of his body. Every thread of will-power, every cell, all of himself.

At the same moment, Jinny heard Doyle shout, 'What are you waiting for?'

There was something in his voice that made her open her eyes. As her eyelids flickered up, she saw the expression on the Hare-woman's face. Only just under control. Balanced on the edge of screaming. And she knew that she had seen that expression before, and very recently. But where?

She nearly did not remember in time, because the similarity was such an unlikely one and she was hunting for pictures of hatred. But, in the last fraction of a second, it came to her. As the Hare-woman's golden eyes narrowed and hardened and her finger moved towards the trigger. It was *Harriet Shakespeare* who had looked like that. Harriet Shakespeare, in anguish because of her love for her son. Without fully understanding, Jinny moved instinctively. She bit Doyle's fingers and jerked her mouth free of them, shouting the words that came into her head. Bella's words.

'It's because you love him that you feel like killing him! But if you kill him, you'll only smash *yourself!*'

The huge eyes widened again, startled, and the Hare-woman looked round, lowering the gun. As she did so, a shot cracked across the ridge, from one of the police marksmen. Putting a hand to her side, she staggered.

Instantly, Doyle let go of Jinny and started forward, his arms outstretched to take the Kalashnikov. But the Hare-woman was too quick for him. Whirling her long, powerful arms, with the last of her strength, she flung the gun in a great arc, so that it sailed up, high above Doyle's head. For a second it was only a black silhouette against the sky. Then it fell out of sight, over Ashdale Great Edge.

As she crumpled, the Hare-woman called into the wind, 'Run, Tug, run! You're free!'

And Harriet Shakespeare, stumbling over the rough ground towards them, raised her voice at the same moment and yelled, 'Tug darling, it's all right. You're safe!'

The sound of the shot blew to Tug on the wind, and then

169

he heard the shouts. Somewhere in the back of his mind he registered that they were both calling to him, Hank and Ma together. But he did not turn, he did not even falter, because his head was up and his feet were pounding. The pain and the wind and the shouts from behind were all nothing. All that mattered was the running, and the voice in his head which sang triumphantly, *This is me. Here I am, Hank. Here I am, Ma. This is me. This is who I am.*